Pancoast's collection is as much full of men and women who have been eaten up--by war, by factories, by life--as it is full of hunger. The tight, terse prose of each story opens up to reveal characters striving for change. Hard work mixes with hard living as bar fights, strikes, and industrial accidents illuminate the lives of the working class. Each of Pancoast's characters wears the yoke of the Rust Belt in a different way--some accustomed, some wild to escape, all working toward some private goal. Pancoast's straightforward, pointed prose fits exactly the hard edges of these characters and the industrial Midwestern landscape in which they exist. *Of Work and War* earns its place in the annals of blue collar literature.

Llalan Fowler
Manager, Main Street Books

Author Bill Pancoast is not afraid of hard work and neither are the characters in these stories. They sweat and suffer for their labor. They are exploited, drained, and depleted. They are pushed to their limits physically and mentally.

War, death, violence, shredded limbs and gutted lives are all covered unflinchingly. Pancoast does not turn away, and he commands your attention without squeamishness or sensitivity.

While the stories of hardworking, blue collar workers in Of Work and War take place decades ago, the lessons are just as relevant today. Readers should approach the book with the same attention they bring to the first day on the job. Open its pages with some courage and apprehension and an earnest ambition to learn.

Alison Shaw Bolen
Editor, SAS

William Trent Pancoast's fiction is an unflinching exploration into the working-class condition. He delves deep, exposing the vagaries of labor and weaving them expertly into a meditation on the residual effects of war. Pancoast writes of big, important issues but never strays from the authentic human experience at the heart of them. Told from a number of different perspectives, Of Work and War is a collection every bit as gritty and tough as the grueling work performed by its characters, but it is not without its share of side-splitting humor and world-worn vulnerability, as well. In fact, it's the many facets of what it means to be alive, surviving, while at constant odds with one's circumstances, that is on full display here, and is the element of Pancoast's writing that perhaps captures most the spirit of a people, and should earn his work a place alongside the great proletarian literature of the past and, quite simply, the great literature of any age.

William R. Soldan
Author of In Just the Right Light

The title of this collection, Of Work and War, speaks to the chronicling of ravages within. Against the backdrop of an America where minimum wage was $2 an hour and a burial would set you back only $4,000, we meet a cast of working class characters struggling with the grim shadows of World War II, Korea, and the Vietnam War. In one story, a war widow works her first grueling shift at a GM plant, while in another story, a young man who dreams of becoming a math professor horribly injures himself rather than go to war. Like so much of Pancoast's work, Of Work and War nets the region's sociopolitical history in narrative: the narrator of "Vietnam. Fucking Vietnam" points us to his father, a WWII vet who "got through the rest of his life by consuming a hundred thousand dollars' worth of alcohol," and in "Virgil's Boy," we find the narrator telling us about miners who "would bury their dead on a Saturday and go back in the mine on Monday." The narrator writes, further, "we worked steady that afternoon, like working people work, one tie at a time, knowing that the job would never be done," and the collection as a whole reads in this way, of an author carefully laying story brick by careful brick, until our understanding of the relationship between work and war is walled into place.

Jacinda Townsend
Author of *Saint Monkey*

In these stories, Pancoast pulls no punches detailing the bone-grinding work of hard physical labor and the war such labor wages on the minds and bodies of those who muscle through it. Pancoast's matter-of-fact prose mirrors his characters' approach to their work and, in true Midwestern form, leaves just enough space for readers to reflect on these characters and their difficult situations.

Gwen Goodkin
Author, *A Place Remote*

Bill Pancoast's characters are frustrated, angry, often on the brink of violence or an insurmountable darkness. Which is not surprising given they have been systematically abused by war and cops and capitalist bosses, a barrage of bad noise. With oftentimes terse and cutting language, Pancoast's is a working class world, one filled with clanging die presses and the gallop of helicopter blades, with revving engines and far off gunshots. It is a world where the war never ended because the soldiers brought it home, tucked like a Buck knife in a leather boot. Of Work and War contains war stories like we've never seen before. It is the saga of the fights that never ended, that may have been hidden but are now exposed. Pancoast's is the voice of the gruff and the gritty, but it is no less compassionate and filled with empathy for the modern day soldiers of the working class.

Nick Gardner
Author of *So Marvelously Far*

Novels by

William Trent Pancoast

Crashing

Wildcat

The Road to Matewan

OF WORK AND WAR

William Trent Pancoast

Blazing Flowers Press

COPYRIGHT © 2021 BY
WILLIAM TRENT PANCOAST
FIRST EDITION
FIRST PRINTING
ALL RIGHTS RESERVED PRINTED IN THE UNITED STATES OF AMERICA
THE CHARACTERS IN THIS BOOK ARE FICTITIOUS, AND ANY RESEMBLANCE TO ACTUAL PERSONS LIVING OR DEAD IS PURELY COINCIDENTAL. HISTORICAL FIGURES ARE ACCURATELY PORTRAYED AND QUOTED.
INTERNATIONAL STANDARD BOOK NUMBER: **9798736390427**
CONTACT: Wtpancoast@aol.com

Acknowledgements

Stories in this collection have appeared in magazines and journals including Night Train, Drafthorse, Revolver, Monkeybicycle, As It Ought To Be, Fried Chicken and Coffee, Steel Toe review, The Mountain Call, Apple, Semaphore, Solidarity Magazine, Working Class Heroes, and The Union Forum.

Folks who have helped me along the way include Moulton DeWalt, Nick Gardner, Amy Greene, Jacinda Townsend, Jim Reiss, Rusty Barnes, Lee K. Abbott, Sheryl Monks, Donald Ray Pollock, Kelli Allen, Alison Shaw Bolen, Okla Elliott, Gwen Goodkin, Denton Loving, Gonzalo Baeza, John Beck, Karen Craigo, Alexander Helmke, David Elsila, Bill Soldan, and all of the gang at Main Street Books in Mansfield, Ohio. My thank you to Alison Shaw Bolen and Nick Gardner for editorial assistance, and to Llalan Fowler, manager of Main Street Books.

For Deby and Eleanor

Introduction

These are captivating tales punctuated by times of war, the overseas conflicts over the twentieth century and the daily conflicts in local communities and industrial workplaces. These stories unfold powerfully in the borderland cities, small towns and hollers of Southern Ohio and West Virginia, an area where rural and urban, factory gates and country roads meet. The overwhelming feeling you have reading this book is the fact that all the men and women on these pages are as real as you and me, that their struggles and joys, problems and dreams resonate and matter with you personally.

Vietnam is featured in many of the stories – the draft hanging over every young man's life, the survival time often measured in minutes for the fresh arrivals on the Southeast Asian shore, and the lingering gnawing of one of America's most contentious wars on the returning veterans. It is not only Vietnam that has framed the lives of many of these characters, however, since service in World Wars One and Two and Korea help to define some of their lives and the lives of their families, both individually and intergenerationally. Though none of the stories in the book are solely centered within the battles and skirmishes of these global conflicts, their presence in the lives of the characters is a shadow never far away from them.

I personally felt these stories ringing true as I turned the pages. My year was one of the last to face the draft though my high number ensured that I was never called to service (though I faced many of the same crises of faith and honor as the men in some of these stories). Many of my classmates came home changed or not at all. Debates about the war raged on long past the final pullout from Saigon and I worked on the shopfloor with men whose lives mirrored those of the veterans living in Pancoast's fictional plants and factories.

It is within the factory walls that these stories give their greatest contribution. The collection tracks the movement between work, home, tavern, union hall and work – as one character in "Navy SEAL" put it, "This was just a job, a place right now to come to between drinks." Though some of these characters are down, they are not often out, knocked around, but not defeated. The stories explore the constant din and oil mist of the factories, places where safety is always a risk, an environment that transforms men's bodies and lives making many old before their time (if they live long enough). It is the rhythm of the line that gives the cadence to the worker's heartbeats and the total of the heartbeats to a life; as Rudolph in "Profiteer" opined about the rhythm, "… hit after hit, grind after grind, shift after shift, day after day, month after month, like the lives of men, every little episode adding up to a lifetime."

The lives of workers are not without conflict both on and off the job. Many of the finest stories in the collection, like "Wildcat" and

"Public Relations," explore the relationship between management, the workers and the unions that represent them. Not all managers are villains since some local managers have a solidarity with the workers they lead, but some through their words and actions make themselves worthy targets of ridicule and worker action (I promise you will never think about a frozen turkey in the same way again, ever). However, though local, some politicians and boosters act in ways that can force us all to question "What side are you on?"

William Trent Pancoast knows this territory, the workers and communities, their conflicts and challenges. This latest book is a worthwhile read and it presented a set of stories and characters that stayed with me long after I turned the final page.

John P. Beck
Our Daily Work/Our Daily Lives
Labor Education Program
Michigan State University

Contents

Salute	1
Vietnam. Fucking Vietnam	2
Virgil's Boy	9
New Hire	36
Home From Vietnam	48
Oxford Town	53
The Mathematician	68
Results	75
Profiteer	81
Navy SEAL	89
Carter	97
Wildcat	115
Pinhead	122
Jim	128
The Rogue	131
Portrait of a Robot	143
Public Relations	148
Hill Tide	159
The Artificial Dick	170
Johnny	179
A Bad Thing	187
Goosy Gus and the Cash Mob	196
The Last Easter Egg Hunt	202
Time	211

Salute

I sit by a window on this twenty-degree-below-zero morning and think what it was like for my dad and all the other kids in the Ardennes trying to dig foxholes in the frozen rocky ground, with other kids trying to kill them through the trees, these eventual men I only knew as stubbled old guys at the American Legion Hall, and how when my dad died in 1979 I had such a bellyful of Vietnam and war I told what was left of his friends that they couldn't come fire their rifles at the grave site, and I think of the concentration camp prisoners forced to go out on work detail in the hard stillness of winter in their ragged coats and flimsy shoes, my dad there to liberate them, and I curse men from time immemorial who have perpetrated such cruelties to other humans; I load my own rifle this Arctic-aired morning, step into the yard and say to the whitened woods before me, "Commence firing," and begin shooting into the trees, steady not fast, the salute that I denied my father, my tears freezing to my cheeks.

Vietnam. Fucking Vietnam

The darkness started on my lunch break at the fender factory. I went out by myself that day, late in February 1980 with snow on the ground, yet with full sunshine, the sort of day that promises something but you know it can't and won't deliver anything. I drove to the local beer dock where I bought the usual six pack then drove back and sat in the GM parking lot with the truck windows down, a cold breeze filtering through the cab.

Down a couple of spaces from me, one of the guys from shipping was sitting in his own pickup and playing Billy Joel's "Goodbye Saigon." He had it turned up loud like you're supposed to listen to that song, the anger of it shearing the hum of the factory in the distance. The song finished and he played it again, louder yet, the choppers, always the choppers in Vietnam, the fucking chopper war, blasting their rotors loud and obnoxious, the anger of the song blending with the arriving blackness of my mood, and it was 1966 again, us high school kids standing in the hallway looking at a picture of a guy who had graduated in the spring, just four months earlier. There on the bulletin board in the hallway was Tom Lane, a little guy, not athletic, not artistic or musical, not handsome, not anything that I could ever remember about him. But he was patriotic and dead. He had joined the Army and gone straight to Vietnam where he got blown up. So the school put his picture on the bulletin board in the main hallway, him kneeling in his fatigues holding his rifle and wearing his helmet, with a caption that read, "Tom Lane, killed in Vietnam last week."

    I sat there in the parking lot thinking of Tom Lane and the next year of 1967 when Vietnam was plastered all over the TV screen every evening, guys getting fucked up in front of us, and a great big What the Fuck was forming in my high school brain. I pictured my dad, the Army Infantry grunt from the Battle of the Bulge who got through the rest of his life by consuming a hundred thousand dollars' worth of alcohol, watching the news, eyes fixed on the little black and white screen but flitting over to me every once in a while like he wondered what the fuck I thought about it, or if I even understood what it was going to mean to me. He never talked to me about Vietnam–what I should do–join up, run, get a deferment, not a thing.

The next year I was a student at Ohio State University. That winter I got a phone call that a friend from high school had been killed in Nam. He had been there a week and stepped on a land mine. His wife was one month pregnant when he died.

I sat thinking these things and seeing these images, thinking too of the day of the Kent State killings when my dad and I nearly came to blows, and a fierce dark anger covered me completely, the Vietnam War upon me again, a sickness that haunted every citizen in America those years–Johnson and Nixon and McNamara sending three million American kids to a worthless jungle just because they could, like the kings of old. Pick a country and make war. The darkness of all things settled over me that day at lunch in the parking lot of the GM plant and I didn't go back in the place that day.

I sat in the parking lot with nowhere to go now that I was back in the middle of the Vietnam War a half decade after the war's end. Back in the darkness, not going down together in Vietnam with my classmates and 58,200 others who got blown up, got sold out by the government, for the glory of nothing. For Nothing.

A whole country with PTSD–the American Legion guys hating the hippies, and the hippies hating the government, the government killing us all, and moms and dads and kids at every crossroad and in every corner of the nation in constant sorrow for the lost or soon to be lost children.

I was plenty drunk, me and several of the regulars–Tony and Big Mike down at the end where they always sat and Crazy Jack three stools down from me–by the time John sat down on the bar stool beside me that evening. I could see that he was half in the bag too. "Hey. How's it going?" I asked.

He just nodded.

"I got this," I told the bartender.

John nodded again.

We drank our beers. I had heard that he was getting a divorce. Him and most of the other Vietnam guys. Treating their PTSD with alcohol like soldiers have done since alcohol was invented. But so was I getting a divorce. So was I sitting here.

"Where you working?" I asked him.

He tilted his head to look at me without turning his neck. "Nowhere man. There aren't any jobs." After a minute he added, "I think you got the last job in America over at General Motors."

"Not much around," I said. I was past the darkness and way into the numbness and wanted everyone everywhere to be forgiven for everything and all get on with America and our lives.

"Your dad said he would get me in the plant. I can't even take care of my family."

"I'm sure he did what he could."

"He promised me. He said it was a sure thing he could get me in."

I imagined my dad sitting on a bar stool beside John up at the American Legion Hall, late in the evening and drunk, treating his own PTSD from 35 years ago and World War II.

"He said us vets got to stick together."

I nodded, starting to lapse back into the darkness from the numbness. "Man, it's hard to get anyone in that place."

"He got you in."

I glanced over at John, watched him rotate the beer bottle and pick at the label, the condensation dripping onto the bar.

"Yeah," I said. The darkness was back on top of the numbness and the anger of Vietnam was returning. I wanted to say I knew what he was feeling, but I didn't because I couldn't. I wanted to say that I was sorry I didn't go to Vietnam, but I wasn't.

"You got my fucking job."

"He did the best he could," I said, thinking of my old man, an accountant who had gotten fired in 1956 for standing up for vets where he worked then, when the company was firing them to beat them out of their retirement.

"Your old man's a liar," he said.

"I don't think so," I told him.

"A fucking liar."

"Fuck you. Fucking Vietnam vet," I scoffed, all the anger and the darkness and numbness all rolled into one big ball of ugliness now.

He was to my right, so when I saw the first movement of his bar stool toward mine, I nailed him with a big roundhouse left hook and knocked him clean off his seat. He got up fast and I was ready, blind to everything except the enemy, and got him another good one. He socked me one hard punch in the eye, then the bartender pulled him off and Crazy Jack grabbed me. He held up his hands, palms out, the dark sadness of the day on him too, and turned and headed for the door.

"What was that all about?" one of the guys asked.

"Vietnam. Fucking Vietnam."

Virgil's Boy

There were fourteen of us on the section gang. I lived in Ohio and I was the only one with a high school diploma. The other thirteen were from Fort Gay, West Virginia, and Louisa, Kentucky, two little towns separated by the Big Sandy above Williamson and Matewan. All the guys traveled to Marion, Ohio every Sunday night or Monday morning to begin their week's work and shared two big old houses near the Erie Lackawanna yards. They shared the house expenses and cooking, took their meals together, went to work every day, and waited for Friday when they could head for home. These were good jobs with union wages. Most years they got laid off for two or three months in the winter so they could stay home with their families.

This was hard, hard work we were doing, hours at a time tamping gravel beneath the railroad ties with stone forks. Before the tamping we hauled the ties up the cinder bank using tie tongs, two men to a tie. Sometimes you just really couldn't get up the bank with two men, but everybody knew which banks those were.

We were the only manual gang left in the state. We jacked the rails up and removed the old ties, clearing away all the rotted wood, replacing every other tie as standard maintenance. After shaping up the hole with a mattock and shovel we'd push the new tie in under the rail. You think it would be close to level and ready, but it never was. Guys liked to do their own prep work, then if they had to tamp too much it was their own fault.

I wanted to be a spiker on the first day there, watching old Willie and Virgil methodically pound the square spikes into the creosoted hardwood. Observing their smooth, powerful swings, much like a golf swing in cadence and timing, I thought it looked like the place to be. When I finally got my chance, mostly to provide entertainment to the old hands one afternoon, I found out different.

If you missed the spike and hit the rail, the rail might split. Spikers worked together in rhythm, one spiked over the rail, the two-inch diameter head of the spike mall clearing the rail by an inch or two. A good spiker never hit the rail. Or you could slide off the spike head and break the spike mall handle. A good spiker left a shiny spot the size of a dime on the rounded head of the spike. Spiking is not as easy as it looks.

It was June 1970 in Ohio where I lived in Marion, not 100 miles from Kent State, where a cruel slaughter had just taken place. Two of my friends had been killed in Vietnam in the last twelve months. As we buried them and the country turned into this maudlin fucking place, hatred and ignorance simmering on the surface, I knew I didn't have any better friends than those two. One of them had gone to Yale for a couple years and then just sat around drinking and smoking dope before he was drafted. He got blown up quick, ten days into his deployment. The other friend was a big, friendly farm boy with reddish blond hair who played tackle both ways on the football team. He could have gone to Toledo and played on scholarship, but he joined up. His brother was a SEAL, his uncle a Marine, so there he went.

I felt lucky to get the job on the section gang. I made enough to pay my way at Ohio State where I had just finished my second year. I chose the section gang over the roundhouse at the Erie Lackawanna Railroad so I could be outside instead of in the dim, greasy machine shop.

I got to know all the guys over the first couple of weeks. Most of them didn't have a lot of education but knew reading was important. I came to understand calling a hillbilly a sonofabitch was like calling a black dude a nigger, and Vietnam permeated the American landscape. It was on all our minds. Take Virgil, his oldest son had been killed in Nam the year before.

Even before I knew that about Virgil, that he had lost his son, he asked me about college– how and when to apply. He wanted to know what I thought were good colleges and how hard college might be. He asked me what a kid should write in the autobiographical essays colleges required.

When he got to the personal part, like how much college would cost, and whether he could afford it, I learned that his other son Andy had just finished his junior year in high school, and at Virgil's urging, was applying to colleges. The boy didn't want to bother with it, Virgil confided in me, but was doing as his dad asked.

He was wide-eyed with the possibilities when I told him I could pay all my college expenses, tuition and food and a place to live, on what I would make that summer on the railroad. I told him they had made the right choice, applying to West Virginia colleges (Virgil was from the Mountaineer side of the river) since tuition was about half as much for in-state as for out-of-state colleges.

"He's got a girlfriend. They're steady together all the time, and that's fine with me and his mother. That's how she and I were in high school. Keeps a young feller out of trouble if he's got a girl. They'll end up married, so we thought it would be best to be close to home. We're thinking Huntington."

"I work during school, too," I told Virgil. "Keeps me in beer money."

He shook his head at that. "Andy won't be needing none of that money."

The more I talked to Virgil, the more I saw how alone he was in his quest to get his boy to college. Not many kids from the hills and hollers around Fort Gay went to college. Many of them went to Detroit or other industrial cities to seek their fortunes. If they stayed close to home, maybe they got on at the power plants on the rivers. Maybe on the railroad in Williamson or Huntington, or even came to Marion, Ohio, to work for the Erie Lackawanna. But in those days such prosperity usually came after they served their country. That was big. All thirteen of my hillbilly friends on the section gang had served, and it was a strain for Virgil to push his boy outside that tradition, especially during war. Needless to say, the body bags made a steady stream to the little funeral homes along the hollers and in the little towns of West Virginia and Kentucky. Their boys were proud to serve and they died in numbers to prove it.

Deferments. Virgil questioned me at length about deferments. "So once he's in college, he'll be exempt from the draft?"

"Yeah. We got that Nixon Lottery now, you know."

"Huh. He'll be eighteen on July 5. Number 188."

"They may not get that far."

"They'll get there. You watch. He wants to go to college anyways."

The weather turned hot in the third week of June, and the boss let us stretch our breaks out a few minutes extra under the shade trees along the right of way or in the shadow of the truck wherever we were working. On one of these extended breaks I realized JB, Virgil's nephew, might be getting a little jealous about all the conversation I was having with his uncle.

Virgil had been telling me about the summer job Andy had gotten, working a man's job cutting right of way through timber for the power company. It was with an outfit that his football coach worked for the first two months of each summer. It paid over $2.50 an hour. We were getting four something on the railroad with our union wages, so $2.50 down home was good money, man or boy. Virgil was sure proud of Andy.

We got a couple of sixty-pound rail jacks out of the equipment truck before our break, and now JB sat on the base of one of them listening from a distance, like he wasn't really listening, to me and Virgil. When we hit a lull in the conversation about Virgil's boy, JB chimed in, "Whitey, I once carried two of these rail jacks a mile to the station. Do you think you could do that?"

I looked through the steamy air at JB. He was dead serious about this claim of manhood superiority over me, and I looked around the group of six or so men within hearing range. They were all looking down at the ground. Some pulled up a new stalk of grass to stick in their mouths, and not one of them cracked a smile or let on to hearing JB's question.

Now I was undoubtedly the weakest member of the gang. These guys all had the ropy forearms and muscular backs their lifetimes of labor had outfitted them with. But no one doubted JB was right next to me in the pecking order. He was one of the younger guys and still carried some baby fat.

"I guess if you could, I could," I said, thinking that quick was the way to dispense with the situation.

My answer cracked everybody up, bringing the guys from a distance to see who or what was being laughed at.

"Old Whitey says if JB can carry two of these jacks a mile, well then, he guesses he can too."

This brought a new wave of laughter and left JB stewing. He poked his eyes over at me once, and I was waiting for that and shrugged real quick, but he looked down again right away. I didn't intend to fuck with poor JB. He'd be taking my spot in last place in the pecking order when I left.

Junior Thompson invited me to join them for a beer that afternoon after work at Deanno's Bar. I had worked with him and Big Willie all day and we talked about beer a whole lot through the heat of the afternoon. We had a lot of laughs over the next weeks, stopping by the bar often. I liked these guys with their plainspoken view of the world.

It was through these stop-offs at Deanno's I learned some of the more personal things about Andy. Junior's wife was first cousins with Virgil's wife, and they had always been close, sharing the details of their lives with each other. Junior was privy to all.

It was intriguing to me when I heard that Andy was planning on signing up with the draft board as a Conscientious Objector. Junior shook his head when he told me that. A CO status wasn't common in the mountains. Seems the boy had become friends with the assistant preacher at his family's church, a young fellow who grew up in Charleston and was just out of Ohio University, and the young preacher had also filed for CO status when he was eighteen.

Some of the information Junior shared was firsthand since Andy and his girl Doreen were frequent visitors at his house. He recounted one evening when Andy blurted out, "Vietnam, Vietnam, Vietnam is all I hear. At the store, on the job, at the Dairy Queen in the evening. So and so's going, been, wounded, killed." All the killing had gotten to the boy, Junior said. He hadn't been able to see any reason he should go half around the world to go kill people who never did nothing to him. After what happened to his brother Allen, sure, he wanted to go to Vietnam and kill every sonofabitch there, Junior said. But the more he thought about it and talked to the preacher, Andy knew the "enemy" was nothing more than a bunch of kids just like his brother that a different government had given guns to and pushed out in front of other kids from other countries.

At least this is the way I pieced together what Junior had told me.

The summer stayed unwelcomely hot, and the pattern of my friends' lives on the section gang lay bare before me as the weeks came and went. Their routine never varied: eat, sleep, work, go down home on Friday afternoon, return to Marion with the sunrise on Monday morning. There were always stories–Grover lost his paycheck in a poker game before he even went home, Big John got drunk and got in a fight and spent the weekend in jail, or there was talk of illness. Cancer seemed to be present in every man's family. They suspected it was from the strip mine runoff throughout the Tug and Big Sandy watershed, but they all supported mining of any kind. They often mentioned in conversation the Farmington explosion of 1968 and earlier disasters in West Virginia and Kentucky and the conclusion was always the same. They had to have their coal mines. They would bury their dead on a Saturday and go back in the mine on Monday. The 1969 Coal Mine Safety and Health Act made it possible for them to continue to believe in the precious black stuff.

Virgil was off work on July 6 and 7 after Andy signed up as a Conscientious Objector, but word made its way to Marion before his return on Wednesday the eighth. His boy was a coward. A Communist. A pansy ass. A draft dodger. The preacher had counseled Andy to help him remain steadfast in his commitments to himself, Doreen, and to God. No one on Earth could judge him, the preacher taught. It was a decision between him and his God. A man's countrymen had nothing to do with his soul.

Virgil got to the station as we boarded the truck on the eighth, and I scooted over and saved him a spot when I saw him coming with his black metal lunch bucket across the cinder parking lot from the train house. The trains were numerous and busy that morning, chugging and snorting and whistling as they coupled and uncoupled, and it was a good thing to have the noise because Virgil didn't have to talk to anyone.

When we got to the job site, Virgil got a mattock out of the rack and hoisted a rail jack onto his right shoulder. JB stood with another jack hanging heavy at his side and a spud bar for prying tie plates. I saw what Virgil was doing and grabbed a shovel, a stone fork, and a pair of tie tongs and stood beside him. He never acknowledged my presence, but he let me help him pull out the first ties when the rail was clear and the spikes and tie plates had been pried up and removed by JB.

Virgil worked as hard as I've ever seen a man work. By 7:30 his blue chambray shirt was soaking wet. He went until nine o'clock like that, me helping him pull out the ties, then him clearing out splintered, rotted pieces and loosening the cinders and gravel with the mattock. I stayed out of his way, just helping him as best I could to get the old ties out and the new ties in. Virgil and JB did the spiking, Virgil hitting the spike head with such force that everyone on the gang stopped and looked to the sound. He let me help with the stone tamping since that was a horrible shit job no matter what your state of mind. He and I had talked enough about Vietnam that he knew I wasn't going to be judging Andy for anything to do with that war.

He seemed to settle in a little at the break. The other guys didn't bother to look his way anymore. By lunch they were occupied. One of them found a bee hive hanging in a little stand of honeysuckle along the right of way and was plotting to take it home, the usual poker game was underway in the back of the truck, and right before lunch was over Virgil looked at me and said, "He still needs to go to college."

We worked steady that afternoon, like working people work, one tie at a time, knowing that the job would never be done. That's the thing about work–it's never done. Pace is everything. There's always more to do just like you've just finished. A worker who doesn't get this can go insane.

It started raining as we got off work at 3:30, a heavy rain, and it kept up all night. In the morning the creeks were swollen to their banks and the rain continued. We hung out in the meeting room for an hour, then a few of us dashed across the black cinder lot to one of the Erie box trucks, got the door up, and sat inside. Several of the guys played five-card stud on an upside-down spike crate. About 10:00 I ran back across the lot to the meeting room and ate my lunch. The boss called it at 10:30. We got our four hours of show up pay.

It rained all Thursday night and by Friday morning all of Ohio was experiencing flooding. We got in the truck and headed out past the switching yard to a siding we had worked on a few weeks ago. There was about five or six hours work left there. It looked like an easy day of finishing it up.

Just after lunch came the news about the washout over past Ashland, Ohio, about 50 miles east of Marion. When it became apparent we were going to the job, we finished up the last few ties and headed back to the meeting room. As I climbed the stairs behind Virgil and JB there was an excitement in the men's voices. When we got settled upstairs and Harry, our boss, laid out the maps, I saw why.

He explained this was voluntary because we would be on the job site for up to 72 hours. Then he explained the pay. We would be on the clock the entire time, with a two hour paid break for food and rest every twelve hours, regular breaks in between the long breaks. Pay would be time and a half all through Friday night and Saturday, with double time starting at 12:00 a.m. Sunday.

We all went home and packed, a change of clothes all we needed since the railroad would have a tent serving meals around the clock–sandwiches, steaks to order, soda, and coffee. The back of the truck was open now as it was late in the day and hot. The smokers rolled one cigarette after another as we traveled east on Route 30 to Ashland. JB finished rolling one and offered it to me. I took it even though I wasn't a smoker. The home-grown tobacco had a strong, bitter taste. I didn't draw too deep or inhale much. I held the cigarette like what looked to me like a joint between my fore and middle fingers. Every now and then I took a hit.

When we got there, trucks were lined up and dumping fresh gravel and cinders for the two dozers along the creek below where the railroad bank had washed out. There was one automated gang setting up on the part of the track that was good before the washout. They set their spiking and cutting machines onto the rails. A hundred men carried tools and equipment up and down the track beside the good set of rails. None of them could do much until our gang laid the ties and rails that would provide the support for the automated gangs.

We got out of the truck and Harry, who had ridden in the cab, was waiting for us with a scribbled list. He broke us into groups of three and told each group what tools to get. I would be with Virgil and JB, and as I hoisted a rail jack onto my right shoulder, JB grabbed another one. Virgil handed me a tamping fork and I followed them along the washout. Guys along the way stopped their work and nodded, a few gave relaxed salutes as if we were in the military. "Guess the work can start now," Harry said to a group and there was much laughing and goodwill at the truth of it. Our bunch of hillbillies was there to go in front of the machinery, make the repairs possible. Without guys who knew how to do it the old way nothing could happen. I was proud to be a part of that.

Of Work and War

The guys didn't let on, just crunched along the cinder bed like we were going to a right of way on a Monday morning over around Marion.

Saturday evening, our break came at 4 in the afternoon. I was exhausted and didn't know how much longer I could go on. I had the option after the two hours to clock out and go uptown Ashland where they had some sleeping rooms for the guys who needed them.

I heard a girl holler, "Daddy. Daddy!" I looked at Virgil and saw a big grin cut across his stubbled face. Past the food tent stood his wife and daughter and Andy and Doreen. He quickened his pace and said, "Come on along, Whitey."

I said I was tired but he tugged my shirt and said, "You'll be alright once you get some food in you and sit a spell."

I followed along and it was then that I noticed Doreen. Her beauty was stunning. A brightness, an aura, emanated from her. I tried not to stare. I looked away and saw that other men were doing the same. Some stared on dumbly. She talked excitedly to Virgil about some happening up their holler and then turned her attention back to Andy. She put her arm around him, drew him close and kissed his ear.

Andy had about him the same extreme energy. He was animated and excited to be a part of this miniature family reunion. He talked with Virgil about the football team. Coach had told him he would be alternating plays at tailback to go along with his linebacker role. Their first game that year was with a big Huntington high school. They usually got trounced, but neither he nor Virgil would accept that possibility. I had played linebacker too and we laughed about the beating linebackers take every game. "My neck still hurts," I told Andy and that made him rub his neck. In hushed tones, Virgil and Andy talked about Andy's CO status. Doreen's dad had a problem with Andy over that, and Virgil said he would run into him at the American Legion Hall Saturday and talk to him.

Andy and Doreen together looked like they were the future of the world.

We had fried chicken and potato salad under the big old maple tree where Virgil's boy had parked the truck. He and Doreen sat on the tailgate and the rest of us sat in folding chairs next to a little table where the food was spread. The food perked me up as Virgil had promised,

Of Work and War

and I observed Andy and Doreen. They were so at ease with each other, young people in love, and I thought of what Virgil had said about young men staying out of trouble when they meet their lifelong love early in life. I flashed my own experiences, picturing nights careening down back roads in a carload of drunks or hiding from the cops when they got wind of our mischief. Watching Andy and Doreen made me happy.

I laid down on one of the quilts they had placed under the maple. When I woke an hour later, it was time to go back to work. Virgil's wife and daughter were up front in the pickup and Andy and Doreen were in the back under the truck cap on the mattress they had thrown in for traveling. I shook Andy's and Doreen's hands and stood at the passenger side giving my thanks to Virgil's wife and daughter for the great meal. Ginny, his daughter, had made the potato salad, and she blushed when I said it was perfect. I left Virgil at the driver's side door and walked back to the tracks.

We worked all night under the generator-powered lights and by Sunday noon I knew I couldn't go much longer. But by 2 pm the job was close to being finished. We were ready to head for home to rest up for the coming week of regular work in Marion.

    I went back to Ohio State that fall. The Friday after Thanksgiving I took off from my job pumping gas in Columbus and drove down to Fort Gay to visit Virgil and his family. When I got there I learned Virgil's boy was living in the shed on his grandpa's hillside farm. He and Doreen were no longer a couple. He had quit the football team. I overheard more of Andy's story as I stood outside with JB and the smokers. Doreen's dad had forced the breakup, all because of Andy's CO status. I knew that a sin of great magnitude had occurred and hoped that Hell was real so that whoever had caused the end of this couple should rot there.

    When I saw Andy I couldn't believe what I was seeing. He had lost twenty pounds and hadn't shaved in a week. He had a dazed look about him and the energy I had seen just a few months earlier was gone. I spoke to him twice but he acted like he did not hear me, like there was nothing in this world he could talk about with me or anyone else. I felt sad seeing him so beat by the things that had happened to him and wished there was something I could do. Andy's sadness made this a sad Thanksgiving for everyone.

It was a warm day for November, and some of the Florida windows on the closed-in front porch were cranked open. The men all sat out there talking and looking out at the tight valley and the steep ridge in the distance. I had expected they lived in a cabin, but the house was a one story ranch Virgil had built himself the year before he went railroading in Marion.

It was still an hour or so before we ate, and one of the women leaned through the doorway to the porch. "Who wants to go get butter?"

Nobody moved. JB finally said, "I'll go."

He got up and said, "Come on, Whitey. You can go with me."

I was intrigued by the beauty of the creek we followed down out of the holler to town and the mountain backdrop. I could see why folks didn't want to leave their homes down in the hills to work in Marion.

JB was over his jealousy, and in between pointing out landmarks in a land he obviously loved, he helped me better understand the situation with Andy and Doreen. That look on Andy was the real look of depression and disillusionment. The timber company had fired him in July and he was working in a little grocery store owned by one of the church members. He rode his bicycle to work. He had quit the football team because of the taunting over his decision not to go to war. He got in fights over it because he was still a proud young man, and one day, standing bloody across from a bloodied former friend in the alley behind the school, Andy dropped his hands and shoulders and walked to his truck in the student parking lot. That was his last day at school. That night he moved out to the shed, away from all he loved and all who loved him.

"What brought it all about," JB said, "was that in October it came out that Doreen was pregnant. They wanted to get married. But Doreen's dad put an end to that idea. He put the word out at the American Legion Hall that his daughter wasn't marrying a draft dodger."

"Then around November first he took Doreen to a doctor in Pittsburgh and she had an abortion. That took the life right out of her. Last I saw her, she looked like the world had come to an end and she's the only one who seen it happen.

"But the worst part is that her dad had Andy arrested for rape. She was only 17, a year behind Andy in school, and Andy had turned 18 in July. Put the boy in jail and it's all been downhill from there. Andy's out on bond now. He'll likely do prison time. Maybe you'll see Doreen. She works part time at the Dairy Bell, where we're going."

In the store a few minutes later, I looked around, hoping for a glimpse of the beautiful girl I had seen a few months earlier. There was a girl working the cash register and another behind the big cooler full of sandwich meat and cheese, but neither was Doreen. JB elbowed me a minute later and pointed to the cooler, keeping his finger by his side so only I could see it.

The girl had chopped dull hair in place of the waves of shiny black hair that had spilled to her waist in July. Black pouches cupped under her eyes, which seemed permanently glazed. There was no trace of a smile. Doreen looked defeated, just like Andy. They were, like true lovers always, I now realized, the source of each other's energy and happiness.

"Hi, Doreen," I said.

She looked up from the meat slicer and I could see she recognized me. "Did you have a good Thanksgiving?"

She nodded and smiled grimly. I wanted to go behind the cooler and reach my hand to her and take her away, back to Andy. This was Romeo and Juliet, set in Fort Gay, West Virginia. What had started as a thing of great beauty had been tarnished and destroyed by scared little men, men who followed the rules of nations and not the eternal rules of God and the universe. But there was nothing I could do.

JB had gotten the butter and other items he needed and was finishing at the checkout.

"I hope I'll see you again," I said to Doreen, and she gave me that grim smile again, her eyes squinting as if to hold back the tears.

We got in JB's pickup and followed the river. "Tough stuff," I said.

"The world's too sad for any of us sometimes, Whitey."

I could only nod. I pictured Andy and Doreen as the couple they had been in July at the washout. When we started up the creek, full from yesterday's rain, it caught my eye, and I watched it all the way to Virgil's.

When I left the Saturday after Thanksgiving I had the feeling Virgil simply wanted me to understand his family's plight, that if I understood it would somehow make things better. I hope it helped in some way that I did understand. My prayers weren't fancy but God had to have gotten my message. I went back to school and thought often of Andy and Doreen and Virgil and the rest of his family. I didn't communicate with Virgil the rest of the year. I met a girl and with school and work I didn't think I had the time.

I returned in 1971 for my summer stint on the Erie Lackawanna Railroad. The guys nodded when I came out of the stairwell at the gathering room, a nod like what they gave one another in morning greetings when they bothered. A minute later JB sat down on the bench beside me.

"Where's Virgil?" I asked.

"He won't be here. Wanted to stay down home with his family."

"He's not coming back?"

"No."

"How's Andy doing?"

"I should have maybe called you, Whitey. Andy killed himself right before Christmas."

I couldn't believe what I was hearing. I once again pictured the boy and Doreen the summer before at the Ashland washout, holding hands like the lovers they were, happy to be alive.

Harry, our boss, banged a toy drum one of his grandkids had given him, striking it once with the wooden ball on the end of a black stick to get our attention. He explained what we'd be doing that day, the safety conditions of this particular stretch of track, that two switches fed into it.

I sat quietly in the box truck as it bounced down the cinder right of way just west of the station. I already had a mattock and shovel picked out. I was going to dig some tie beds. They would be just the right depth and width and the ties would slide in just right.

JB must have seen what I was up to because he was right behind me with a rail jack and gravel fork and tie tongs. I worked steady till the first break, soaking my blue chambray shirt like Virgil had that day last July, sweating out the poisons from within, the poisons of war and hatred and ignorance that none of us could ever escape. I could never get all the ties put in, never be finished, but I worked that day like it was possible.

New Hire

Kay's dad had told her the night before that she shouldn't go in the GM stamping plant. "It's no place for a woman," he had said.

But she felt like she had no choice. No place for a woman? Was there any place on earth for her? Ever since Carl had been killed in Vietnam two years ago, there had been no place for her. Would this country provide a place for her? For her and her daughter? Not likely. The $4,000 in life insurance barely covered the funeral expenses. She was living with her parents. And now, after working at the garment factory for a year and a half, she had heard that General Motors would be hiring the first women into its Cranston stamping plant. All she knew about the place was that it paid $5 an hour and would provide insurance benefits for her and Carla.

Carl had been drafted into the Army right out of high school. If she had known she was pregnant, he would not have been sent to Vietnam. As it turned out, she conceived on his

Of Work and War 37

last leave the week before he shipped out. Kay still didn't know she was pregnant when she received word of his death three weeks later. She went about burying him in a cloud of pain and grief. She still could not remember parts of that time. There was the funeral and all the friends from her high school class–the other cheerleaders, the boys who had played on the football team with Carl, and some she didn't even remember.

She and Carl were so occupied with each other in high school that there were many classmates they never got to know. Between every class, they would meet under the stairwells or in the corridor between the cafeteria and the gym, and hold each other, making their own reality in the midst of the childishness of high school. All they ever had needed was each other.

Today, inserting the hard plastic earplugs as she had been instructed earlier, she wished Carl was here with her. This was a noisy, unfriendly place, and she and the other eleven women, the first ever hired for factory work here in Cranston, eyed the confusion swirling around them. As she walked onto the plant floor, she heard shouting from behind and was alarmed at first, thinking that someone was hurt. But as she and the others soon found, the shouting was just the catcalls and whistles that seemed to emanate from every corner of the smelly, barren place.

Tow motors, platform trucks, and fork lifts raced by the women, the drivers craning their necks to get a better look. The women followed their corporate guide along the congested aisles, stopping now and then as the guide deposited them, one by one, with white-shirted foremen. Kay was shown to a line of car door outers streaming in an unending line down a conveyor belt. The stacker tucked the door panels together and stashed them in an orange cart. The foreman left her standing there with the man and she watched him, trying to see how she could manage to do what he was doing. Shouldn't they have asked her if she could do this job? Maybe asked if this was the job she wanted to do? But no ... the man showed her how to snap three of the doors together at their corners, and she put on her thin cotton gloves and learned what she had to learn in order to survive in this place.

The doors came so fast that she did not know what to do with them, and then they were sliding off the conveyor and onto the floor, and the foreman was there shouting at her, and she could see men beyond the huge, sweaty whiteness of his shirt laughing and pointing.

When the fallen doors were put away and the conveyor started again, the panels started coming. She was ready and fought for all she was worth to see and feel how these heavy, slippery pieces of steel fit together and went in the rack beside her. In a half hour, the cotton gloves were shredded and turning red from the cuts on her hands. The humidity of the day engulfed her as the temperature passed 100 in the plant, with no fans anywhere to stir the heavy, oil-laden air, and her tears and sweat mixed together, blinding her. She fought the panels for hours, oblivious now to the catcalls and insults from all around her, and somehow made it to the lunch whistle. She couldn't remember the way out and stood fixed in place.

The 90-plus-decibel noise of clatter and clang had been replaced by a humming noise–all the electric motors of the presses idled in place as the half hour lunch break came. She started in the direction of the only women's restroom, a hundred yards away. All the way there she was followed by the catcalls and whistling, and took the time now, as she walked along the main aisle, to look to the sources.

"Hey, baby. How about a blowjob?" called a middle-- aged man who elbowed his partner on a maintenance cart. The other man was embarrassed now that she was looking at them and nodded to her. Then she felt a slap on her ass as a cart came whizzing by within inches of her.

She could not go on and found a place to sit on a guard rail, watching the insanity of this place in disbelief. Maybe her dad had been right. This was no place for a woman, this place full of lunatics and leering men who acted as if they had never seen women before. She thought then of Carl. He would have beaten these people up. No man would ever have dared to treat her this way when Carl was alive. And the thoughts of Carl gave way to the thoughts of her daughter Carla. Nothing would change the facts of her plight since Carl had been killed. She was the one who needed to be strong to take care of Carla. She was the one who now had to make a living and provide healthcare for her daughter. With the girl's breathing problems and asthma, the medical bills had mounted, and Kay already owed over $6,000 to the hospital and doctor. The family doctor had told her not to worry about the bills, but she still got one every month. The hospital was threatening legal action. She wiped her eyes on the sleeve of her blouse and stood up. Now that she was off the line, she felt some strength returning to her, and as she started up the aisle once again, she felt that Carl was walking here with her, that the mental picture she had of him would protect her.

By the time she reached the sign pointing to the restroom, her tears had subsided. She descended the stairs to the press pit, where the only women's restroom was located, feeling as alone as she had ever felt in her life. She stood before the huge metal wash trough, not remembering how to even turn it on. She stared at her reflection in the steel mirror on the wall above and barely recognized herself. Her face was streaked with dirt and oil from where she had rubbed the tears and sweat away. Her blouse was pulled half out with an oil splotch down the middle. And as she stepped back and looked down to her feet, she saw that the oil stain covered her down past her thighs. It was itching, burning her now that she had the time to recognize the feeling. She lifted her blouse and the skin of her stomach was red from the door panel solvent. She opened her jeans and peered under her panties, and she was red all down her front. She buttoned herself back up and accidentally stepped on the water activator on the floor. Glad for this simple pleasure of running water, she washed her bloody, torn hands, the powdered soap stinging the wounds, then began splashing cold water onto her face.

Shortly, she had washed her face and was peering once again into the mirror, patting herself dry with a paper towel when she heard the women's voices. "Bastards," she heard one of them say. And another, "I think I broke my fucking hand." Then there was laughter as several other women came into the restroom. "You hit him a good one!"

Kay glanced away from the mirror. She looked rough. And then she noticed the others looked beat also–they were disheveled and sweaty and dirty like she was. They jabbered among themselves as they washed up, and some of them sat on the benches in the restroom, the only safe place they knew of in the forty acres under roof, eating their lunches. Kay did likewise, glad for their company, and pulled her bologna sandwich out of the children's lunchbox she had picked out at the Uncle Bill's discount store the evening before. And before she had eaten her cookies, the three minute whistle blew and the women trooped up and out of the hideaway and back to their jobs.

Once again came the catcalls and whistles from every shadowy corner of the plant. But by now most of the women knew what Kay had learned–that the men would shut up with a glance in their direction. And as the ladies peeled off from the group and went back to their jobs, they exchanged barely perceptible touches and pats from each other–maybe only the fingertips brushed at the arm's-length end of a wave or a hand against a shoulder, a solidarity they could not yet name but felt.

And then Kay was there again, at the end of the line where the car doors would soon approach her at a speed of 8 doors a minute, one every 7.5 seconds, 480 solvent-dripping, steel car doors every hour. Another whistle blew and the place exploded with noise over the next few seconds, every press starting up again, every conveyor rattling on its sprockets. She barely had time to pull on her oily, bloody gloves and begin defending herself against the onslaught of doors.

She wanted to cry again. The first few doors reopened the wounds on her hands and the oil burned her stomach and thighs, and the sweat blinded her after a couple of minutes. She had forgotten to reinsert the earplugs, and the noise was painful, hurting her ears, her feet hurt from standing in one place so long, and she had blisters on her heels from walking in the rough leather work boots purchased when she bought her little, blue lunchbox the night before. The minutes went by, and then an hour had passed, and Kay wanted to lie down and sleep, but the doors kept coming, seeming heavier and heavier so that she had to force herself through each lifting movement. She wanted to quit, but she knew that by lunch today she had already made $20, an amount that would have taken her nearly two days to earn at the garment factory. Her daughter needed for her to have this job. She needed to have this job and its earning power if she was to get back on her feet and have a life again. She would die in this stinking, horrible place before she would quit. The tears came and mixed with the sweat and oil and grime, and she stacked car doors.

When she thought she could not continue for another minute, when the doors were indeed becoming too heavy for her fatigued muscles, she felt a tap on her shoulder. She turned and there was the black man she had noticed earlier in the day as he ground steel at a work bench along the door line. He motioned for her to let him take her place and handed her a folded up piece of oilcloth. As she moved aside she accidentally kicked the foot control, shutting the line down.

He turned the line back on and she watched, trying to learn how he did it, as he snapped the doors together and slid them into the slots in the orange cart. She unfolded the oilcloth and found that it was a makeshift apron fashioned from the material used to shield the aisle ways from welder sparks. She had noticed other workers wearing the bright blue material earlier, and now held it up to herself and slipped the top string over her neck. The cloth draped easily down her front, and she tied the strings of the homemade apron behind her back.

Her foreman loomed up the aisle, charging towards her position at the door line to see what had cost him a few car parts in his little world of noise and steel. And then beside Kay were two other men–Milt Jeffers, the union's shop chairman, and his sidekick the production committeeman. The chairman glanced at her bloody gloves and nodded to the stacker, then stepped on the foot control to shut the line down. The foreman continued toward them, though by now his approach was downright sheepish and tentative. He had been told by upper management that the women must survive; he would be fired, he had been warned, before any of the women hired that day were fired.

Then Milt was shouting at him, and pointing at the conveyor and then at Kay. The anger of earlier was replaced on the foreman's face by a look of terror. He knew he had made a mistake even coming over to the line. Earlier he had noticed her bloody gloves and had not acted. He could have helped the girl, but he needed the parts for his quota, always the quota, the only thing that mattered in this place, his boss pushing him to do more than was possible, the car parts valued more than life itself.

And then the break whistle blew and Milt shouted, "You'll do what the fuck I tell you to do." His voice seemed to echo in the sudden quiet and several men gathered around to see how this situation involving the powerful shop chairman and the production foreman would play out.

Milt turned back to Kay. "Let's see your hands." She pulled the oily, bloody gloves off and showed him where her hands had been cut by the panels. Even though the wounds looked a horrible mess, she didn't feel any pain.

"You walk her up to the plant hospital?" Milt asked the man who had helped her.

He nodded, motioned for Kay to follow him, and off they went. She looked back once, saw Milt Jeffers pointing at the line and shouting at the foreman again, and smiled her first smile of the day. Management was the enemy. The union was her friend.

Home from Vietnam

Steve Brown stood at his job in the pressroom loading door inner panels into press P3, the blanker presses nearby banging so hard they shook the entire forty acres under roof. For a while every morning at the stamping plant, Steve was agitated and dizzy like he always got in Vietnam when mortars were incoming.

The pressroom was in full motion, the draw dies at the front of each line whoomphing as they pressed the metal into its various shapes. The trim dies could be heard breaking metal, with trim pieces clattering down the scrap chutes. The hem dies did their clump, clump-clump dance hammering panel flanges from every conceivable direction. The gap presses on the quarter panel lines added their own special explosions each press cycle.

Steve loaded panels, one after the other, 660 an hour, and grew numb to his task, wishing by eight o'clock that he had a beer to go with the Bennie he had taken at daybreak to get him up and into the plant for his Saturday shift that paid time and a half. The fog of noise and oil mist drifted over him, just like the dawn mist and the last few C-40's of the night in a rice paddy in Nam would have a few weeks earlier.

He still wore the Vietnam suntan, dark over all his body except for his skivvies lines. He should maybe have taken a few months off, but knew he would have just drunk himself to death. He had gotten home, signed in at the plant office, and was back to work a week after he had stepped out of the bush in Nam.

Steve hadn't slept in three nights, had sat up drinking beer, popping the Bennies and acid he got from the longhairs in the plant. Strange, him just back from Nam and the only people he could relate to were the kids who were against the war. Nobody in their right mind was for the war. Not now. He still wore his fatigues, but only because they were the clothes he had that fit him. Some of the older guys thought it was because he was proud. He wasn't proud of anything right now, not a fucking thing he could think of, and wasn't even sure he wanted to live. Nothing in his life made any sense.

This place was pure bullshit, but it was something to do, something to get him off the couch above the garage at his parents' house and out into the world. They couldn't understand why he didn't want to sit with them on Thanksgiving Day and talk about shit with his sister and her family, her gung-ho kill-a-gook husband who had never set foot out of the states in his defense services job.

He had sat the night before watching the news, watching the rerun of his buddy Tinker getting blown away as he ran for a helicopter two months ago. He couldn't believe it–folks at home watched the same shit night after night, not even knowing they were watching reruns.

The line was running good today, and if the P line workers ran rate they might have an hour to get a nap, or get in the eternal poker game in the cafeteria, or more likely, go through the hole in the fence and walk the quarter mile through the woods to the Roundup to get started on the nightly drunk.

At lunch time, Steve ran the well-worn path to the bar, first man to get there because of his conditioning. He had two shots and two beers, and was feeling much better about his life when he reentered the factory. On his way back to P line one of the longhairs slipped him a blotter, righteous blotter acid, maybe from the master Owsley himself. By twelve-thirty, the stinking, noisy fender factory was looking mighty fine. The noise was music now, and the oil mist was the fragrance of industry and prosperity for all. But then the line went down. The foreman got Wimpy the die maker, called Wimpy because he looked like Wimpy in the Popeye cartoons, to put his gin and tonic down and diagnose the problem–a broken trim steel– and the line would be down the rest of the shift.

Now they would get beat out of the hour they had coming in rate for busting their asses all morning. There went their nap time and their drinking time. The foreman set the men to work cleaning up, and gave Steve a chisel to pry slugs out of the tar-covered wood floor. He took the tool and tried to make sense of being on the tar floor of a factory in 90+ decibel noise prying metal slugs.

Thanks to his sedation and training, he adapted, squatting and prying with the chisel, stacking the slugs into three piles–one inch, three-quarter, and half inch, with the smaller slugs in a haphazard pile. He imagined it a game, and was doing fine until the foreman came by and kicked all his slugs toward the scrap chute. He looked up and saw the smoke of battle. Then over by the tree line, where Tinker and Doper were on lookout, a C-40 exploded.

    He clutched his chisel and crawled along the press line. Ah, good, somebody had called in the coordinates, and the napalm was already dropping. The fire and smoke filled the air over behind V line where a group of automatic welders was operating. Tinker and Doper hadn't returned fire, and Steve knew they were down. He would crawl the rest of the way to the hole they were in and bring them out.

    The foreman's kick to Steve Brown's rump while he was peering through the smoky haze of the battlefield brought him to his feet like the wiry animal Nam had made him. He sprang and slashed with his knife all in one motion, cutting the foreman in the chest, and then turned and dove into the tree line. Steve Brown landed in the midst of the automatic welders. There was no fire and smoke the next weld cycle. The war was over for Steve Brown.

Oxford Town

Cindy came breathless from running and stopped by my desk in the laundry office.

You need to come quick. Jimmy's gone crazy.

I saw the fear in her face and got up and followed her the hundred feet to the bank of commercial washing machines lining the wall of the plant. In front of the bleach barrel Jimmy stood with the bleach paddle cocked like a ball bat ready to hit the other washman Samuel. It was a hot September day in the laundry where even in winter the temperature would be over 90 degrees.

Jimmy had looked a little drunk when he came in but I hadn't cared. I'd have been drunk at this place too if I could have been. As I neared he kept hitching the paddle back behind his right ear like he was at bat. Samuel had his eyes locked on Jimmy's and I figured he would do a takedown when the swing came. Samuel had been all Ohio in wrestling and at tailback for the Talawanda Braves in Oxford, Ohio.

Excuse me I said to the ladies in the circle around the two washmen when I pushed past. There was me and six or seven black girls from the neighborhood down the hill on the north side of town and five hillbilly ladies from the countryside plus a couple of Miami University coed dropouts stuck in Oxford like lint on a piece of laundry.

Give me the paddle I told Jimmy. He dropped it several inches right away and I could see in his eyes that he was relieved. He knew Samuel was going to kill him if it came down to it and he handed me the paddle making sure I was between him and Samuel.

I knew that the paddle was a lightweight balsa sort of wood and wasn't going to hurt a whole lot even if somebody got hit with it. Not like it was oak or ash and heavy enough to bust a head.

Go clock out I told Jimmy. He was sobering up now from the adrenalin and backed up a few steps then walked up past the office to the time clock. It was silent till he was gone then the black girls gathered around Samuel. The football coach had told him to put on 15 pounds of muscle and get in top shape along with getting his ass enrolled at Miami University and he would let him walk on next fall for a tryout if he had a C average.

You're a hero one of them tossed my way. The others murmured assent knowing that if Jimmy had swung the paddle they and Samuel would have been blamed anyways since black folks in Oxford Ohio in 1974 were still used to taking the blame for most everything involving conflict with white folks.

I was half crazy from lack of sleep and the workload I had taken on. I was doing my student teaching all day and managing the commercial laundry on second shift. The college and my sponsor teacher had told me I couldn't do what I was doing and I'd said okay and went ahead with it anyway. What were they going to do? Throw me out of school because I had to work my way? My days started at six in the morning and ended after midnight.

All I wanted was for these folks to get the fucking laundry done so I could be finished with work for one more day. I didn't even have time to drink anymore. I was surrounded in this college town by beer and drugs and pussy and I spent my days with a classroom of eighth graders then tons of bloody hospital laundry from Dayton Ohio.

Let's do the laundry I told everyone. They grumbled as they made their ways to their assigned work areas. The first loads of hospital gowns from the dryers had just hit the folding tables and I put half the sorters over there. The big steam roller press we ran the sheets through was running good tonight. All eight of the washers were churning suds except for the cavernous four hundred pound capacity behemoth that Jimmy had been pulled from and tossed like he himself was a bag of laundry across the concrete floor.

He had called Samuel a nigger then made the mistake of turning back to his work of stuffing a fifty pound mesh bag into the washer like it was business as usual after the insult. I have no doubt that Samuel also called him a cracker before it was over. I didn't give a fuck. There was laundry to be done so I could go home and guys calling each other crackers and niggers I didn't have time for. Somebody somewhere along the line should be responsible for telling all humankind that some motherfucker sooner or later was going to call them a cracker or a nigger or wop or dago or a sonofabitch and that the correct response was to grin and walk away. But no. Young men and old men had to beat each

Of Work and War

other with bleach paddles and other blunt objects when somebody called them a name. Sticks and stones motherfuckers.

They were all back to work and I headed to the office and tomorrow's lesson plan. We were going to listen to Richard Nixon's resignation speech from the spring of the year. Classic dipshitese. There would be a writing reaction to his speech and I was jotting down topics when Cindy was back again breathless.

Jimmy's mom is here.

From the doorway came the gruff voice of Jimmy's mother. You the manager?

I am the tired motherfucking manager I wanted to say but instead said yes maam.

I learned in the next fifteen minutes from Jimmy's mother that Jimmy was a fine upstanding youth with a family to support and he damn well needed this job and she damn well expected him to keep it or she would use her considerable clout as assistant head of housekeeping of women's dormitories on the South Quad to damn well make my life hell at Miami University.

We had walked out of the office to the laundry area and she kept looking down the aisle at Samuel and he kept track of where she was looking and I wished there had been some gravel to kick. They were the Oxford Henleys I was told. Generations of them had lived on the same farm and little Jimmy was destined for some form of great bullshit. I took in all she was saying. I didn't want trouble with anybody.

I never aspired to be a laundry manager. I saw an ad in the Oxford Press for second shift help for minimum wage at the Oxford Laundry down the hill on College Avenue. I didn't realize till I got there that it was a commercial laundry. They did one hundred per cent hospital laundry that I was soon to find was gross as punctured intestines. There were sometimes slivers of flesh or body parts wadded up in the sheets. Mostly the laundry was just bloody.

I helped at the horrendous job of sorting. Helped with some of the shitwork. Showed the ladies I was one of them. And got them started on it. They would stand and look at it somehow thinking they could avoid what they knew they had to do. All of them had to say eww at least twice and examine each basketful as if sizing up the enemy.

I said let's sort this shit and grabbed a tangle of gowns and surgical garb and they squawked like teenagers which half of them were. The black kids were all under age 20 and the white ladies were older picking up a few bucks for their families for Christmas. Whenever possible I assigned the older folks to this job. Having learned that bulling ahead was the best way to deal with bad shit in life, they would get it done quick.

It was a nice June day when I applied for the job. My breath was sucked from me when I entered the place. Heat radiated off every item in the plant. Washers and dryers, steam boilers and presses. But I came to find that it was a dry heat like they say Arizona has and was something a person could adjust to.

Minimum wage was $2 an hour. That would feed me. I had a thousand dollars saved up from my stint as a salesman and needed to get through another nine months. Turns out they were putting on a second shift to take care of a contract for a Dayton hospital and the owner wanted me to be the night manager. I had wanted to work about twenty hours a week but he offered me $200 a week salary. I could hardly turn down a job in a college town during the Vietnam War at two and a half times the minimum wage. I took the job and it nearly killed me.

My lesson plan was finished and I was helping Samuel load the washers. I enjoyed hefting the floppy fifty-pound mesh bags into the openings of the washers. It was good exercise and I didn't have to do it if I didn't want to.

I felt responsible for the mess with Jimmy and Samuel. The washman duties amounted to a person and a half job and we had two people to do it. They had been alternating on the shitty part of the job with one of them at any given time sitting for extended periods while the other worked. The boss had noticed this when he stayed over a few times and told me he wanted them busy. So I told them to work together thinking that they would only make each other miserable. Not get stupid about it.

I tossed a bag into the medium washer in the middle and saw a man enter the rear of the place through the fire door. He headed for the little roller press where Darlene was feeding pillowcases and an argument ensued. Darlene was one of the hillbilly ladies. She seemed glad to be here at work every night and did a great job helping get the laundry done and me home.

She rolled her eyes and shook her head no while tugging tangled wet pieces out of the basket.

There's no fucking supper I heard him say.

She was telling him what was at home to fix for him and the kids and he stood looking down at the gray enameled concrete floor.

I took a step closer and he turned toward me. And you better just stay the fuck out of this he said.

Before I could react to what he said Darlene cut past me and was pleading for a few minute break to get her goofy half drunk husband out of there.

No problem I assured her and headed back to the washers. I kept my eye on them near the back door and in five minutes all the shouting was over and he stood looking at her with his lower lip quivering and I swear he wiped a tear from his eye before she pushed him out the door into the parking lot.

Darlene hurried over to me. Thanks she said. We need the money from my job. It won't happen again.

I stood nodding my head and watching her hurry back to work. With an education she would have made a good nurse or maybe a teacher. Folks worked hard. Everywhere I've ever seen it's the same. People hump ass all day and night whatever it takes to make a living. Better than growing turnips for the king I guess but the workers always seem to get the short end of things.

I smelled John and turned to find the old man leaning on his broom. He was a human cloud of BO. Hot tonight he said blowing the sweet scent of Boone's Farm Apple wine over me. That's good wine he had told me one day. Better than that rotten Mogen Daven he called the MD 20/20. I didn't have the heart to tell him it wasn't even real wine. But Boonie's was pretty friendly stuff for a dollar twenty-five. In high school we called it liquid acid. A bottle of that stuff would set you free. Sometimes I envied old John his daily Boone's Farm.

John had been a medic on Guadalcanal. The first 24 hours left him crusted in a layer of blood and dust and sand and he had started shooting up with the morphine from the emergency kits of the dead men. It was the only way he could keep going and do what a man and a soldier needed to do. After that he would never again go another day without being fucked up on drugs or booze. Settling on the Boone's Farm as he entered old age was probably one of the better choices he had made in thirty years.

The evening was moving along nicely now. The last of the dirty stuff was in the washers. The workers were all doing a great job. I hadn't had a chance to talk to Samuel and didn't really know what to talk to him about. Today was payday and every payday Thursday I treated myself to a pizza and some beer. The laundry paid in cash and I fingered the $157.36 in my pocket and envisioned the pizza. I headed back to the office thinking maybe I could get a little nap.

But first I needed to sketch out the rest of my courses to complete my Masters Degree. Miami had developed a program to lure folks like me with a BA in English to come and take a few more English courses and the usual lame ass education courses in order to allow them to step inside an Ohio classroom.

So I was mulling over my choices and thinking about how I was even going to survive the next eight weeks of 20 hour days when Cindy -stood breathless again by my desk.

She leaned close and said Samuel's uncle is here.

Henry was a little shorter than Samuel but twice as wide and his breath smelled like garbage. I could not imagine what cheap form of whiskey could smell so foul.

I'm sure he had a noble purpose when he made plans to intercede at the laundry after he and the rest of the neighborhood heard of the fight. But now that he was here he didn't seem to remember why he had come.

Samuel my nephew he said.

I shook his hand and it was like grabbing hold of a potato masher all hard and so big around I didn't feel his fingers.

Equality he shouted belching a fog of garbage gas over me. We been through a lot.

I looked at Samuel to maybe see a way out of this but Samuel seemed as scared as I was becoming.

Justice the uncle thundered and brought his right fist down like a pile driver on the stainless steel work table buckling its center and leaving it concave.

I stepped back as much to get away from the stench of his breath as anything and he stepped right with me.

It ain't agonna happen again he said.

This was a big man. Probably 350 pounds and not a lot of fat. I learned later that Henry had played defensive tackle for the Steelers in the mid-fifties.

Henry's growling and thumping went on for another five minutes until Samuel's aunt got there and started slapping Henry in the back of his head. Then she had the bleach paddle that had ignited this whole mess spanking his backside and chasing him across the floor as he held his hands over his ears and tumbled out the back door into the parking lot.

I looked at Samuel and he shrugged and I shook my head. I sat along the wall for a few minutes watching the folks work. Cindy was by herself pushing full baskets to the back of the plant and this told me the rest of the folders were sitting. Let them sit. Let the workers of the world sit when they can I decreed.

It was after eleven when I went out and fired up the box truck and backed it to the loading dock. Tonight three of the black girls volunteered to help push baskets and racks to the dock. Samuel and I sized up the load and got started.

I had always tried to be fair to Samuel and Jimmy. They were different but both were honest and did their jobs. We were about half way done loading the truck when I asked Samuel what happened.

He called me a nigger.

And?

I grabbed him.

You made contact first?

He was drunk.

Yeah I said.

I wish I could have sat Samuel and Jimmy down together. It would all just have been all right. They both would have jobs and be moving ahead in whatever they saw as the paths of their lives. But Jimmy's mother and Samuel's uncle had muddied that up. I didn't ever want to see any of them again.

After we had finished and stood leaning against the dock I told Samuel this was his last night too.

He figured that was coming from the conversation we had had while loading the truck and nodded.

I heard the girls arguing about what kind of three two beer they were going to get at the carryout. One of them had her dad's pickup and they were going spotlighting on the road to College Corner to see what was out in the country at night.

I shut down the boilers and locked up. Down the block I stopped at Domino's and ordered a pizza. I drove out to Millville where I bought a six pack of real beer and drank one on the way back to pick up my pizza.

The Mathematician

In high school, Dana was on the math team, one of only seven members the year he was a senior. Algorithms, calculus, trig functions, and advanced geometric configurations were the language he spoke best. His math teacher said that Dana had one of the best analytical minds he had ever seen and should apply to both Case Western and MIT.

His dad had laughed at him. "Hell, you're an idiot! College? You can't even build a fucking dog house," he had shouted at Dana, referring to his attempt to build one so he could get a dog when he was eleven years old. The old man had bought him a four by eight sheet of plywood and some two by fours and nails and set the wood up against the saw horses in the corner of the garage. Dana drew a picture of the dog house and would go out to the damp, dark garage every day after school. He even cut the two by fours in half to make them easier to deal with, but the handsaw kept getting stuck in the plywood.

It was about this time, after the dog house defeat and after his mother left home, that Dana started walking with his head down. Folks mistook him for a wizened old man when they saw him shuffling along, never looking up, like he carried a great weight on his thin, young shoulders. It wasn't until he met algebra a couple years later that he snapped out of his physical slump and began walking upright again. Math was something that felt good and true, just like he imagined it would have felt to have a dog when he was eleven.

He had been somebody for a while. He always got the top scores in math on the Iowa Basic Skills Tests, and scored in the top one tenth of one per cent on the Merit Scholarship tests. He would be a professor, maybe, or a scientist. But his dad just laughed at him. "Shit, boy," he would holler at him and hold out the big roll of money he carried in his pocket at all times. "Here's what it's all about!" And the old man would point out the back window of the dilapidated farmhouse to the junkyard he had made out of the forty acres he had inherited when his dad died.

Dana's dad was rich. He worked second shift, seven days a week at the stamping plant and ran the junkyard during the day. When the boy was a senior in high school, his dad gave Milt Jeffers, the shop chairman at the GM stamping plant, $1,000 to get Dana a job when the company was hiring again. Sure enough, by the fall of 1969, Dana had been hired, and had become a full-fledged autoworker. Once again, he started walking with his head down.

Then in the spring of 1970, he found love, got laid, got married, and he straightened up again. She was a kindly, plump girl, as happy as Dana was to have found someone, and she didn't see any reason he shouldn't check into going to college part time and studying math. There certainly couldn't be any harm in it. So he had enrolled in the regional Ohio State campus in calculus, and was scheduled to start in the winter quarter of 1971.

But then had come the draft notice just before Thanksgiving in 1970. "Viet fucking Nam," he had muttered over and over as he and his wife sat at their little kitchen table, and he drank beer for only the second time in his life.

"It's time for bed, dear," she had finally said, as midnight approached.

"Viet fucking Nam," he had answered and passed out on the table.

Dana started walking with his head down again. He would never be a college professor. He would never win the Fields Medal. He would never do anything but stack five thousand door support panels every day for the rest of his life. His fate was unthinkable, and he hatched a plan, which, if successful, would not only keep him out of Vietnam but put him in college fulltime on the way to fulfilling his destiny as a mathematical genius.

He would get hurt at work in order to make his plan a success. If he were permanently disabled, he could collect Workman's Compensation benefits, or even Social Security disability benefits. For days, he imagined the various ways he could get injured–run over by a tow motor, his foot caught in the conveyor track, crushed between a rack and the press, his arm tangled in the parts conveyor–he would figure something out. But after a week of flirting with tragedy and death, Dana had gotten nowhere. He always stopped at the last moment before walking into the aisle in front of a vehicle, and the one time he forced himself to carry through, he got honked at and told to get the fuck out of the way. Another day he tried to cut his hand off in a press, but only got grease on his shirt before he pulled his arm away. Disabling himself was proving to be more difficult than he had imagined.

On the Saturday after Thanksgiving, Dana decided to walk into a scrap chute. He didn't know how badly he would be hurt, but some of the guys who had fallen in got pretty fucked up; one had been killed, but Dana was sure that could not happen to him. Right after lunch, he abandoned his post and walked across the aisle to the quarter panel line. Phoomph. He fell faster than he had thought he would. Immediately he was struck by the putrid smell. Then he felt the sharp scrap pieces cutting him. He cried out, but it was too late. More pieces came down on his head, cutting his scalp. Then he got stuck, and the slime from the panel lube was suffocating him as he struggled. After a full minute in the bottleneck at the bottom of the chute, he came piling out onto the conveyor belt in the basement.

He was coated in blood from head to foot. He tried to get up and off the moving conveyor belt, but kept slipping and cutting himself even more. Then his conveyor hit the main conveyor. He had to get off this thing. Hadn't anyone seen him fall, he wondered? He made one violent lunge to try and roll off the conveyor and onto the concrete floor six feet below, but his leg was stuck. Dana realized he might die. And he wasn't ready to die. Better to die in Vietnam than in this stinky, slimy pile of scrap.

He passed other conveyors feeding into the main one, like so many small streams feeding into a river. And the conveyor was getting wider. Shit. The baler house was another thirty yards away. He pulled himself up and looked ahead at the scrap metal feeding into the compartments and being squashed into two-foot cubes. The noise was deafening, and he knew that no one could hear his yelling and crying, yet he kept it up, tugging at his leg, which was now held fast with the frayed wire of the conveyor belt deeply entwined in his blue jeans. He forced himself onto his side to try and get his pocket knife out.

He was on the final uphill run to the baler house. Then he felt the pain. A scrap piece stuck along the side of the belt sliced him, and he looked down, his crotch already red from the gushing blood. He lay back and waited for death, suddenly calm. Let death come, he told himself. Maybe he could get a dog in heaven, or puppies even.

The bailer house crew was tidying the place up for the next shift, and Howard was getting ready to toss the day's trash into the compactors when he saw a big red thing on the conveyor. It was a body! Howard hit the E-stop and yelled for the others, then called the maintenance base.

The millwrights were there within five minutes. When Dana saw them he hollered, delirious now with the loss of blood, "My dick's cut off!"

He said it a second time and one of them slapped him with a greasy pair of leather gloves. "Shut the fuck up. Your leg's cut is all."

Results

I had just gotten notice that my latest story had been accepted by Prairie Schooner. I was breathing rare air as I hurried up the street to meet my brother for a beer. No corrections were suggested by the editor and none had been made by me after the first writing. A one draft story, maybe the best story I had ever written. Now that was what I would call results.

I reached the saloon before John, and took a booth halfway along the right side. Just after I sat down, two young guys wearing Cranston letter jackets came in. Cranston was the next town over, and the rival of my hometown of Oakridge in football.

I had just gotten our beers when John pushed the heavy wooden door open and squinted into the semidarkness of the place. He too was wearing his high school letter jacket, 12 years after graduating, and started towards me. I noticed the two Cranston fellows pointing at John and laughing. He slid into the booth opposite me and I was glad he hadn't seen them.

"Big Brother," I said, "I've got some serious results to share with you." I had taken to calling him that when I was twelve and he was sixteen, when he was this giant guy on the football field on Friday nights.

"Glad somebody has results. My dump truck caught on fire today. I lost four hours pay and I might get fired. What you got results about?"

"Results" were always what our dad said he wanted. He didn't want just efforts, even the best we could do. He wanted results. The word had just sort of stuck with us, Dad dead for many years and us knowing he never meant anything but the best for us when he said "results."

"Oakridge," I heard one of the Cranston boys snort. Then laughter.

John turned to look their way, then turned back to me.

"I just heard a while ago …" I started off but was interrupted. "Hey, old man, what you doing wearing that shit rag?"

John didn't miss a beat. "Pipe down, sonny. We're having an adult conversation over here." The two picked up their beers, glaring in our direction, and I tried again, "My latest story …."

A peanut hit John in the head. Before I could say anything more a peanut hit me too.

I watched my brother, his lips puckered out like he was pouting. He really couldn't do anything about these guys. Last time he was in a bar fight he broke a guy's jaw and one of his arms. It got ugly in court, and the municipal judge told him he never wanted to see him again or bad things would happen.

The right side of John's face twitched a few times. He would kill these punks if that is what it came down to. He'd always been a big boy, big for his age, bigger than all of his classmates. Coaches used him. Taught him how to hit hard early. Hitting hard hurt, no matter how old or big you were and he was fourteen when they started banging him against eighteen year olds.

Now as I watched him trying to ignore these shitheads, I realized these things. They had used him because he was born big-boned and good-natured. The concussions had piled up, and by the middle of his senior year he was finished. Oh, they got him a custom-made helmet, mostly to make the coaches feel good about themselves, and used him on special teams till it became obvious he could no longer risk even that limited exposure. Then he was finished, slower but the same good-natured big kid. A year in Iraq sucked more of the life from him. I remembered how sad he was after he came back home, always looking quietly at the floor.

I needed to get him out of the bar and drained my mug. "We can drink a few at Mom's later, huh?" I said and stood up. He poured half the mug down in one swallow and pushed himself from the wood seat. I had to piss bad, so I said I'd be right behind him.

I was almost done when one of the Cranston guys pushed into the restroom. I was no fighter and didn't know how I was going to handle this. But I was also no coward. While I stood pissing I was thinking about Townie, the memoir I had just finished teaching the prior quarter. If you know you're going to be in a fight, for sure, no way around it, get the first punch in. End the fight with one punch if you can.

I stood washing my hands a minute later. I was scared. What if I hit this guy and it didn't even hurt him? I remembered that part of the book too, Andre Dubus III always sizing up guys he might be in a fight with. The punk bumped up against me at the sink. "Pussy," he sneered.

Of Work and War

I finished rinsing the soap off my hands and a strange thing happened. I knew I was going to clock this guy. I knew I was going to knock his teeth down his throat. He was to my left and I watched his eyes in the mirror. When he glanced away from me I let him have it, a combination hook and right cross from waist level with my body behind it. I caught the right side of his forehead, must have got his temple, because he dropped to the tile floor.

I stood drying my hands with a paper towel, keeping right behind the door. When I saw the movement I slammed into the door with all I had, heard the clunk as the other guy's head hit the door jamb, and that fucker was down too. I threw the paper towel at the first guy on the floor, then got scared again and backed out of the restroom. I walked through the bar smiling. The adrenalin was still pumping and I felt like I was walking on air

Big Brother was waiting for me outside by the curb. Later we would meet at our mother's, him with his wife and three little ones. "What results you got?" he asked as we followed the curb to the bar parking lot.

I felt my bruised, maybe busted, middle knuckle of my right hand and winced as I straightened the finger. "Nothing, Big Brother." I would just send him a copy of the magazine when it came out several months later. I would leave it up to him whether getting a story in Prairie Schooner counted.

Profiteer

Rudolph trollied the gantry crane from the die car to his work bench, stopping near the spotting press to let Charlie, his work partner, move out of the way. "The chains are manmade," he always said of the crane safety rule about carrying a load over anyone. Weak link, weak chain…if only the affairs of men could be so easily understood. The spotting press bottomed out, an apprentice making one of thousands of hits necessary to spot a die to its finish, hit after hit, grind after grind, shift after shift, day after day, month after month, like the lives of men, every little episode adding up to a lifetime.

As he stood waiting, Rudolph harrumphed to himself over the inferior tool room here at GM. Back home before the war, ninety per cent of these die makers would have been fired for their slowness or incompetence. But, ha, he laughed to himself then: this big, slow meandering industrial machine of America had been good enough to defeat Germany.

Rudolph was talking to himself again. He didn't like doing that, but more and more there were discussions occurring in his mind. He had hashed most things out again and again, always coming up with the same conclusions: that he was becoming an old man, that his children and grandchildren and soon to be great grandchildren were doing well, and that he was a very rich man with the machine shop that he ran in Cranston and the seven-day-a-week job here at the stamping plant. He could retire, but there was something inside him that would not let him walk away from such easy money as the factory provided. He had known hunger. His family had been hungry after the war and during the transition to the new world, first to Canada and then to Ohio, USA. In every instance it was his status as a tool and die maker that had allowed him to provide both for his family here and his relatives left behind.

And now, after all the tragedies that war had visited upon the Motherland and the world, time after time, age after age, as if to prove the stupidity of man, this new war, this Vietnam, was happening. And it was making him wealthy beyond belief. And wasn't that what wars were about? Money? He felt the one ounce gold coin in his pocket, his "just in case" coin that he had carried for twenty years, just in case a calamity should occur and separate him from home and family one more time before death. His wife and children and grandchildren also all carried a one ounce gold coin at all times, at least they said they did, but he knew they sometimes found his gold coin plan amusing and left the gold at home. Let them think what they like–the day, God forbid, might come when an ounce of gold bought a tank of gas to flee to safety, or bread to stave off starvation. He had seen it and lived it. In the safety deposit box, along with lots of cash, were two hundred ounces of gold.

    He would be ready if and when this land of plenty was plunged into the darkness of war or famine. And wasn't that his role as patriarch now that he had seen the greed and evil of men destroy civilizations, countries, and the lives of man? To be ready in case of darkness of war so that his offspring could survive? What he knew about the pitiful and precarious state of mankind was simple–given the right conditions, lack of food, clothing and shelter–men became animals, and their savagery was unequaled in the animal kingdom.

    His daughter had been on the outskirts of

Dresden after the firebombing. The little girls and all the young women had been hidden away as well as possible from the Russians, while the older and wiser females fared as well as possible through the rampant and brutal rapes. She had never talked about it, but he knew. Just as his time at the camps was something his own mind kept hidden from him, his daughter's mind must also have hidden the horrors from her and her generation. Indeed, to go on, one must attempt to put those things of the war behind and bury them forever.

He had watched the beginning of the war in Vietnam, studied its tactics and needs, and taken the gamble and invested in the huge automatic lathes and boring machines, turning out shell casings twenty-four hours a day, seven days a week, to be used to kill the enemy. The government contracts were lucrative and profitable beyond belief. His shop had gone from thirty employees to over three hundred since 1964. In the last few years he had managed to save, after taxes, several million dollars.

Finally his way was clear, and Rudolph trollied the crane to his work bench. He set the 20,000-pound die shoe on the steel horses, walked to the bench, and poured himself a cup of coffee from his thermos. Then, sitting on his metal stool along the wall, under the huge set of blueprints for his job, he closed his eyes. The wars were never far from his mind, even after all these years. He had been only a boy for the first one, seventeen years old, and ready to die like a man, but he knew, all through the year he spent in the trenches, trembling and cold at night, fearing death, that he was no different from boys of all nations sent to fight and defend their countries in the name of God and patriotism, when in fact the reasons they were fighting were money, pride, narrow self-interest.

    Rudolph sipped his coffee and remembered his childhood friend Wilhelm whom he had held dying in his arms shortly before the end of the first war. Why was his mind forcing him to see these long-forgotten pictures of cruelty and pain, he asked himself, starting yet another conversation within. Had he not put to rest the hunger and violence and the mindlessness of war many years before? Had he not suffered enough of war than to sit and think about it? He avoided memories about the second war, a war in which his wife and one of his sons had died. His time at the ovens was something that he was able to mentally retreat from, what he had done too ghastly for even the mind of a killer such as himself to ponder. His family did not know. And even now, here in America, he knew that if his presence could ever be connected to the camp, he would be tried for war crimes.

He stood up to pull himself away from these thoughts and began unhooking the chain from the die shoe on the horses. His partner Charlie had gone to wash up for lunch, and he sat back down, all of a sudden tired. His American wife had been after him to retire, and he had begun thinking about it. If the company knew how old he really was he would have to retire anyways. But he couldn't stand to be around his bumbling fool of a son-in-law, who ran the plant for him. He could not hurt something as profitable as the business, but Rudolph hated to watch inefficiency and stupidity at work, and could never keep his mouth shut. Better that he stay here at the fender factory to pass his days.

He thought of his grandson William, the best hope to carry on the business. The boy was a good mechanic and studying mechanical engineering at university. Rudolph remembered with amusement that when the boy was home from college last summer, he and some friends had organized a march against the war in Vietnam. They marched in the Fourth of July parade, carrying their homemade signs. Rudolph could have been proud of him were it not for the absurdity of what the boy was doing–protesting the war that was paying for his college and all the nice things he took for granted, protesting against the spoils of war, the shell casings made in the machine shop of his grandfather.

Rudolph leaned back against the prints, twenty sheets of them making a cushion for his head, and dozed off. He woke twenty minutes later to a slap on the shoulder.

"Come on, Rudolph. Let's go. Another fucking wildcat."

Rudolph muttered as he forced himself awake. Another strike. Fools, he thought. He looked up to the speaker, a young machinist who was one of the few to ever stop and talk to Rudolph. He accepted the hand held to him and struggled up, locked his tool box, and fell into line in the aisle. He had never liked that word, "fuck," and wondered why Americans were so fond of it. "Fuck," he muttered to himself. What a meaningless word. As they neared the exit, Rudolph reached into his left pocket to finger his gold coin, but couldn't find it right away. Frantic, he felt every corner of the pocket. It was gone! His one ounce gold coin was gone! He turned to go back into the factory to look for it. Everyone and everything was flowing toward the exits. The forklift driver never saw Rudolph as the old man came running around the blind corner in search of his gold.

Navy SEAL

Lee strode down the wide aisle behind the press lines. He was a few minutes late in getting to his work area, which was the farthest from the time clocks, but he did not hurry. The smirk on his face, a combination of mischief and boredom, had been his trademark ever since he had completed Navy SEAL training in 1967.

When he had reached the work area, Lee draped his wiry frame over the foreman's desk and waited for the bald, little man to look up from his paperwork and begin his daily bitch about Lee's work habits. Sensing Lee's presence, the little man looked up, scowling. "I've warned you before about being late."

Lee stood immobile, still smirking. "This is serious," Smitty said.

Lee let a smile curl the edges of his smirk. This was not serious. Getting shot in the ass was serious. Swallowing the sewer water of Hanoi Harbor was serious. This was just a job, a place right now to come to between drinks.

The foreman ranted, and Lee once again pictured the gruesome task of his SEAL Team. When he hoisted himself out of the murky water, the killing had already begun and there was blood everywhere. There were 13 Chinese advisors aboard the ship for R&R, and the mission was to slit their throats without making any noise. There were a few, muffled cries from the young prostitutes as the SEALs went about their work, and soon they stood in a perimeter on the main deck of the boat, looking into the darkness for their ride out.

"Follow me," Smitty ordered. "You get here late, you get a shit job."

Lee shuffled along behind the man, his lankiness hiding the steel cable muscle sheath around his skeleton. Shit job? He chuckled and wanted to stop and talk to Marie, who was busy chucking panels into her small press. They had been together for the first time last night, and her welcoming love had given Lee the first feeling of hope he had had since getting back from Nam three months ago. Instead, he winked at her and kept on behind Smitty.

In a minute, they had arrived at the X line. In X2 was perhaps the largest die in the world, a Cadillac roof trim die for the new model year. The pad had been sold off for bearing the day before and was now ready for clearing. The normal procedure was to pull the die out of the press, flip the upper shoe, pull the pad, and grind the clearance with the pad setting on the plant floor. Or, the whole die could simply be flipped and left in the press.

"You can thank your union for this fine job," Smitty chortled. "The die setters refused to come down this aisle last night, said there were safety issues," and Smitty laughed, the first time Lee had ever seen the man show any sign he had a sense of humor. "So you get to grind it overhead." And Smitty wheeled and was gone.

The first thing Lee did was lower the palm buttons to his chest level. The second thing he did was open up a scrap chute and place cardboard over the gaping hole. And the third thing he did was saunter back up the aisle to Marie.

His smirk disappeared and became a wide grin as he approached the petite, dark-haired girl. That had sure been fun, spending the night with her, and he couldn't wait for quitting time so they could hop right back in bed. Marie saw him coming and her rosy cheeks curled into little balls as she thought back to the previous day. She liked this stoic man. He didn't talk a lot of nonsense and needed her as much as any man had ever needed a woman. She could spend the day with Lee lying on top of her, fucking and sleeping and fucking again. Lee knew he was being shadowed by his foreman so they couldn't talk long, and in a couple of minutes Lee was on his way to the home wok area to get his tool box.

"Hey, Muledick," he heard as he came around the stacked dies hiding the entrance to the work area. A couple of journeymen and a new apprentice sat drinking coffee in front of their tool boxes, their little metal stools lined in a semicircle so they could shout over the noise of the low-ceilinged, small press area to each other. Bill, the apprentice, looked toward the approaching man—he had heard stories about Lee, the Navy SEAL that no sane man ever messed with. But even when he had drank or smoked or snorted himself into a stupor, Lee had no meanness toward his often bellicose, fellow drunks.

In a few minutes, Lee was on the way back to X2, pushing the heavy, steel clad Kennedy and machinist boxes past where Marie was rapidly pumping the press pedal, hoping to reach rate by early afternoon. This time, Lee only nodded and pressed on—it was time to get set up and get to work. Back at the line, he parked the tool box and went about putting the die blocks between the upper and lower die shoes. He didn't know why they bothered to block such a massive die. If the press decided to cycle, it would squash the blocks and squirt them like missiles across the plant floor. The upper weighed forty tons and the upper pad, suspended on die pins, itself weighed fifteen tons.

He attached the long air hose to the press air fitting and set up his six inch grinder, looked down the aisle, winked at Marie, put on his face shield and respirator, and crawled into the die. The big grinder torqued heavily, and Lee braced his right arm against a die post, throwing the cast iron sparks in an arc of fire across the aisle. In a few minutes the metal dust began building up on the die and floor beyond, and on every square inch of Lee's body, seeping into his lungs even through the protective equipment, and covering his face in black soot.

Lee ground hard for an hour, finishing one side of clearing, until his arm muscles gave out. He laid the bazooka, as the giant grinder was called, across his chest and gazed up at the die.

He chuckled to himself, thinking again of Marie. Then he fell asleep.

Just before the 9 o'clock break, Lee woke to a string of profanity from around the front corner of the press. Foreman Smitty had driven up the aisle on his golf cart when he saw Lee sleeping on the job. He parked the cart and speeded up his attack, motioning to another tool and die foreman across the way as he moved in to make his bust. He had the goods on Lee this time and would wipe that smirk off his face.

But then as Smitty had charged forward– BAM—the palm buttons hit him square in the forehead. He spun around, dizzy, looking for something to hang onto, yelling "Fuck!" over and over and then as Lee came fully awake, staggered across the front of the press bed and as Jeff, the other white shirt arrived, Smitty disappeared.

Lee disconnected the air hose from the bazooka, climbed down off the trim die adaptor, and tossed the air hose onto Smitty's cart. "What's up, Lee?"

"Not much, man. How's it going?"

"Okay … how you doing? Get rested up yet?"

They both laughed. Jeff was a marine who had served from 1967-1969. He knew Lee from the American Legion Hall–they had both sat there at "last call" at various times in the last few months–and they both knew that "rest" would be a long time coming for most of them, and may only come with age as it had for many of the WWII vets they drank with on a daily basis.

"Where's Smitty?" Jeff asked then. "He was here just a minute ago."

Lee looked around. "I don't know. He was here ... I heard him cussing about something."

The break buzzer blew, and Lee hurried down the aisle to wash up. He and Marie were meeting at the break area.

Smitty climbed the stairs from the press pit back to the pressroom. He could have died! The slime from the scrap chute made his shoes slippery on the stairs. He was bleeding from scrap cuts in three or four places and his glasses had snapped in half where the palm buttons had banged his forehead, and he was having trouble seeing. He staggered up the aisle to his golf cart and sat there looking around. He still didn't know what the fuck had happened to him, and put the cart in gear to head up to the hospital.

When he had gone thirty feet, he hit what felt like a patch of oil and the rear wheels spun on the tar-covered wood block floor. But they didn't let loose like usual and kept spinning. Smitty was pissed. He floored the accelerator and the cart crept forward, the wheels still spinning. Then the air hose that had draped itself around the rear tubular bracket of the golf cart frame pulled out of the air fitting on the press and Smitty was propelled, wide-eyed, past the press line and across the main aisle. Workers ducked and ran out of the way as the cart smashed into the far wall at the quality department, where Smitty finally knocked himself out.

Carter

This town got any good pussy? was the first thing I ever heard Carter say. New hires Jerry and Carter had joined us on a job 100 miles northeast of Columbus seeding a golf course and there they were at 7:00 a.m. planning their evening foray into the little burg up the road.

I could use me a fat little momma.

Squeeze your dick so hard she'll bring tears to your eyes.

That's the one I'm looking for.

Let's get this show on the fucking road then.

The show was the first flatbed of straw we would be working. It had barely got below 80 overnight and the bales radiated the day before's heat. Jerry and I would be hauling them to load the straw blower Carter had lucked into operating because of his small stature. Old John would be spraying seed with the water cannon and the boss's son Jake driving the tank truck hooked to the flatbed and blower.

Jerry had joined the Army in 1956 when he turned 18 his sophomore year of high school and spent a year and a half as a cook before being tossed for shooting smack. He never did figure out how it happened. Mostly just fell in with that crew from the Bronx. But he couldn't kick it when he got back to Oakridge Ohio and it didn't take long for his clumsy burglaries to lead the police to him. He ended up spending two years at the barbaric reformatory in Cranston. After that ordeal he was clean and hardly ever ventured past beer in the drug world. Now he lived at home with his old man whose hobby used to be beating the shit out of his kids when he got home from the bar every night. But now he was burnt out and disabled from the booze and cigarettes and steel mill.

Carter was just a badass. He wasn't a big guy. Five-eight maybe 165 pounds. But he would climb you like a monkey with oversized arms punching the face or back of the head at close range while he held on to the neck. Every bad dude has to kick a cop's ass and he had done that when he was 21. Nobody that knew him bothered to fuck with him anymore.

Carter and Jerry laughed more that morning than I had heard of laughter for the last five years with a machine gun barrage of jokes and ribbings and pussy rants. I found myself drawn to them yet I sensed the danger there. A person might venture too far into their fantasy world and maybe never come back. I just knew I needed to hear what they had to say about their world and the plentiful pussy there.

And then there was just work itself that led me to have enough respect for their world to enter into it. I had become a working man by age twenty as much as I could say that I was anything. I was intrigued by the antics of Jerry and Carter and impressed with Carter's charisma. I would be one of them.

The first night we went into town around eight in Carter's '56 Ford. A souped up black coupe, and he would bet anyone $5 they couldn't snatch a five-dollar bill off its dashboard while he was accelerating. I got to sit up front since Jerry and Carter had taken a liking to me because neither one of them had ever known anyone who was going to college. I laughed and started to say bullshit but only got the bull out before Carter slammed that baby in second gear and plastered me to my seat. We had picked up a twelve pack and the beer was going right to our heads with the heat and it seemed funny to all of us. I never felt anything like that I said. What the hell kind of motor you got in this? Jerry was laughing harder than any of us and kept saying over and over you didn't fucking believe it did you Whitey? They had taken to calling me Whitey when they first saw me that morning because of my blond hair.

Jerry slugged down his third beer through his laughter and became more animated. By the time we had found the only bar in the crossroads town of Weber and ordered a pizza from down the street Jerry was getting bug-eyed and happy as hell.

That day on the golf course had wasted all of us. I had lost eight pounds according to the scale at the truck stop we were sneaking into for showers every evening. By ten o'clock I saw that I wasn't going to be able to keep up with these guys. Nothing was happening at the bar and when I razzed my new friends about the loud-mouthed frizzy-haired lone female in the place they assured me the good pussy would be there later. I set off on the mile walk down the country road to the golf course where we were sleeping in a barn used for machinery storage.

We had set up cots in the barn and even with the end doors open to catch whatever breeze there was the place was hellhole hot. I sat on the end of my cot thinking over the day. Might have been the hardest day's work I had ever done. It ranked right there with the hay-baling I had done a few times. This was a prevailing wage job since it was all municipal and state projects so I could make enough money this summer to pay all my college expenses. I climbed in my sleeping bag and closed my eyes listening to the crickets and some night birds I couldn't identify and smelling old manure and oil and grease. I felt a plop on the edge of my pillow. I inched my hand over and felt the fur and then came the flurry of bat wings as the sonofabitch took flight again. I pulled the bag over my head and passed out.

Rise and shine motherfuckers was the first thing I heard in the morning followed by time to shit shine shower and shave. Laughing I pulled the covers off my head.

Good pussy Whitey. You should have stuck around.

Jerry and Carter were already dressed and getting it together for another day in the field. I had to hurry to avoid being left behind as Carter revved that big old motor and spun the tires in the gravel just outside the barn. Jake and John were staying at the motel beside the truck stop and we met them for breakfast there. Jake was getting ready to finish his MBA in the fall and all he could do was bitch about having to work every summer in order to get his college bills paid and a wad of cash in his pocket for beer and girls at school.

At breakfast Carter got to talking about a Beagle he had growing up that had dug holes all around its dog house to stay cool in weather like this. It lived its entire life except when it was taken hunting chained to an eyebolt on the dog house in the backyard. After Carter had done six months in the pen for the cop beating he moved in with a girl who had been introduced to him during a visitation with her brother. Her place had a fenced in backyard and he moved his fourteen-year-old Beagle there from his mother's backyard. The first weekend out of prison he spent building a dog house. He figured the old girl could make up for lost time in this clean and safe new home. But she fussed over her surroundings laying pained by arthritis in the opening of the new lumber-smelling structure just like she still wore the chain and never strayed 10 feet from the dog house. Carter had to move out after a couple months when his girlfriend discovered what an incurable cockhound he was. Left his old dog because of the little girl who loved her then got a call that she had snapped at the three-year-old. He went and got his dog and took her out to the reservoir where he held her underwater. I just wanted her to feel what freedom was like Carter said and ate his pancakes.

That day was hotter than any I ever remember in my entire life. We sweat so much and then quit. Our skin got dry and clammy then we sweat some more. Jerry was having trouble picking up the bales by lunchtime his hands were so swollen and blistered through the cheap cotton gloves we had picked up at the truck stop. The sweat dried in salty circles around our eyes and the straw dust coated all the skin bared. Every now and then Jerry or I would collapse on the trailer bed and wait for the energy to return then get up and go another round with the bales. They got heavier and heavier as the hours passed. I thought hard about how it would be to have this to look forward to all my life. Shit work in the hot sun. Jake was riding in the shade of the truck so he didn't comprehend how the sun was draining us.

At the afternoon break at 3:30 we had about 35 bales to go on the second flatbed. Jake wanted to go until seven so we could finish up early on Friday and he could get home to his girlfriend. I was watching Jerry when he heard the suggestion and saw him shudder. He and Carter neither one were in a position to call it a day. John sat stoically listening. He would do whatever the boss told him but you could see the numbness in his eyes.

We were all in pain and I guessed it was up to me to save us. Without a union there weren't any rules in our favor. Suppose we just finish that load and call it a day? I said.

We need to get this hole done today Jake said. John? he asked the old man who was really the brains of the outfit.

John had been at it for thirty years with Jake's dad who was a small, sickly man who had figured out how to bid on state projects from books in the library. I never quit he said. But I've had enough for this day.

We quit at 5:30 and the last thirty minutes into the new trailer of straw Jerry was happy as hell. Don't get any better than this he said and I saw that the impending cessation of pain was what he was referring to. Looking forward to cooling down and getting a shower and having a few beers to save our lives from this inferno. We maybe weren't a whole lot different from Carter's dog I thought one day years later mulling over that day of my life. Maybe all behavior is about escaping pain.

I got a nap in an easy chair near the trucker's lounge after my shower. That and a steak dinner at a Lake Erie marina restaurant twenty miles to the north had me feeling like a human being again. We hit several honky tonks on the way back south after supper. At the last one when we walked into the chill of a fully cranked air conditioner Jerry elbowed me. There you go Whitey.

Carter led us to a table with three college looking girls. I followed along. Then he leaned forward with his Popeye forearms bulging toward the girls as he placed his hands on the table. Ladies this is your lucky night. Whitey here is God's special treat for the female species.

After buying me and the girls enough beer to get us half drunk Carter winked at me and he and Jerry left.

I'll take you home said the one I had taken a liking to.

Next morning in the barn I woke to Whitey got him some pussy!

I wasn't going to tell them I didn't.

The little blonde with the nice titties!

Brunette with the hairy box!

Mostly we talked about sociology. She was also majoring in it at Ohio State in Columbus.

After breakfast I was in the truck with Jake going to help fill the tank with water and mix the grass seed. The old tanker bounced down the fairway to the water tipple by the railroad and I braced myself to keep from banging my head on the window.

You and that ex-con were taking it pretty easy yesterday. I saw you laying around back on the flatbed.

I looked at him through the morning haze the temperature already bumping 80. Bullshit.

Bullshit? I saw it. I don't know why the old man keeps hiring these fucking bums.

Jake was cute. Dimpled cheeks, unworried face. He had been five years ahead of me in school and drove a new red '57 Chevy convertible and had a pretty girlfriend to ride around town with him. Us younger kids would see him at the root beer stand or the drive in. He had been somebody we wanted to be.

But now as I looked at his perfect profile in the morning sun I hated him for the spoiled punk that he really was. Nobody was fucking off on the flatbed yesterday.

He jerked his head to look at me. I say you were. Ex-con fuckoffs and you.

Fuck you.

He was pissed because he had to be here with us bums and pushed his right fist over the seat space and caught my chin. I gave him back a right cross and he leaned away then grabbed me in a headlock. He was strong from playing football in high school and college and I couldn't get away. I started punching him and he tightened the vise. When we hit a big rut his grip loosened and I hit him in the nose and he let go.

Fuck you. I'm quitting. You're an asshole.

No no. I need you here.

I saw that he had quickly realized he would be shorthanded and not be able to get the work done for the rest of the week.

Double our breaks. Two in the morning and two in the afternoon. No work after three when it's so hot.

He stared at me with the spoiled jock anger jumping out of his dark eyes. Yeah. Yeah okay. Four though.

That day and the rest of the week passed a little cooler. With our extra breaks and one early quit day we all recovered some and added a little weight back. Jerry was a lost creature with a big heart and I liked him. Friday afternoon the talk turned to getting home and ready to party. Be at the Grotto Jerry told me. Good time acoming!

I had never been to the Grotto which was an uptown bar full of what us kids had always called greasers losers hillbillies. When I got there about eight the place was noisy and teeming with the Friday night worker crowd. Standing at the end of the bar was Jerry all lit up and bug-eyed and off to the races. This was what he did now that his life was straightened out. He worked hard long hours without the desire or knowhow to get rich and then he got fucked up and had a good time with the money that he had earned.

Standing with him was a chunky girl with a white halter top which glistened in the strobe lights that activated when the band played. Jerry waved me over to join them and hugged me into the girl who had turned to face me and now had her breasts squished into my stomach. Man this is Gina he yelled above the noise of the music and squeezed us harder. She grabbed my dick and then squirmed back towards Jerry.

The evening was a blur with Jerry buying drinks for folks he knew and spending up the paycheck advance he had gotten earlier in the day. I cashed my check and bought us a couple of rounds. Carter got there about ten and it was then I found out that Gina was his girl. She whispered into his ear and he winked at me guess you two already met and slapped my shoulder.

Carter could dance and he got Gina sweated up and sat her down and found a fresh one and kept going. He was smooth like a gymnast in movement and strength. It was after one when they started on the Bacardi 151 lighting it on fire before taking the shots. I had been trying to leave for a couple of hours but now my evening was escalated as I took my turn at the shots and did two that I remember.

Then it was closing time and Jerry said we're going swimming you're driving and I was jostled out the door by six or eight of the friends I had made that night. I got in my '51 Mercury and sat in the relative quiet of the parking lot listening to cars starting and revving and Jerry said follow that Studebaker and I put it in gear.

I wasn't fit to be driving and was all over the road. I had heard of the place we were headed. An abandoned quarry about eight miles out of town but guys in my generation had never partied out there. It all seemed like a bad idea. Jerry was still cranked and he just shook his head no when I asked if we could call it off. Always got to finish he said.

When we got there and had started along the path through the woods we heard the splashing and yelling from the wide expanse of inky water barely lit by the half moon through the haze of clouds. Gina was the only girl there and she strolled among the naked guys half of them strutting around with hard dicks.

Jerry was stripping down dropping his clothes in a pile. Come on he said.

I took off my t-shirt and dropped my jeans and there was Gina in front of me. Before she could grab my dick again I dove off the bank and joined the others in the water. The chill of the quarry finally cooled me after the week of heat and I treaded water watching the goings on around me. Carter was behind me huddled in the water with one of the guys.

Then we were all on the bank getting dressed. I pulled my pants on and Gina put a lip lock on me and grabbed me again. I heard Carter laughing off to the side and then he slapped my shoulder. Good pussy he said leaning into my ear as he and the other fellow bumped past. Touching Carter's girl scared me and I stood still with her hanging on to my rear belt loop.

I smelled weed then and took a hit when it came my way. Another hit and I realized how drunk and fucked up I was. We were all on the dark path again and Gina was hanging on to me and it became apparent that she and I were leaving together. I heard Jerry jabbering and he joined us at my car.

I was out of the parking lot first and gunned it to show off. Nearly lost it and headed back to town. I was having trouble seeing now and wondering what the hell I had got myself into. I had a little hillbilly girl hanging on to me. Jerry was talking a mile a minute like maybe he had gotten some speed in him.

I was going too fast when I came to the curve a mile from the quarry and the right front wheel went off the right side of the road. The berm was deep and when I pulled back the steering wheel jerked out of my hands and banged my wrist. Then the car veered clear across the road and I slid into deep grass that grounded my frame and stopped us like a parachute would then spun us loose in a circle. I felt Gina sliding away from me and grabbed her arm then watched as Jerry slid out the passenger door that had been jolted open.

I got stopped and sat in the quiet then saw the headlights behind me. My door was jammed so I pushed Gina out the door and slid across the bench seat. A couple other cars pulled alongside the road and in their headlights I saw Jerry lying at the base of a tree. I got there at the same time Carter did. He turned Jerry over and it was obvious his neck was broken. Blood covered his scalp and his eyes were still bugged out.

Gina get in my car he said.

Carter's face was calm and lit up by the headlights behind us. Whitey it's been nice knowing you.

I had no idea where he was going with this. Was he going to kill me after what I had done to Jerry? Man I'm sorry I said.

Shit happens. You get in your car and get the fuck home. You weren't here tonight. No one ever seen you.

But Jerry. The truth is ….

There ain't any truth one way or the other about this. There ain't anything true or false anywhere I've ever seen Whitey. Stuff just is. I'll take care of Jerry.

I stood and backed through the group and Carter and another guy already had Jerry picked up. They laid him in the trunk of the Studebaker.

The cars were pulling out and heading back to the quarry. Carter leaned on the window of my old Mercury. Get you lots of pussy Whitey he said and was gone.

I drove slow on the way home. The way I should have been driving earlier. But I was in a different world then.

I didn't go back to work the next Monday. I had enough money saved up to get through the second summer session and fall and winter quarter at Ohio State. I got a room on 12th Avenue and dug into my studies. In the fall I looked up that sociology major from the honky tonk and ended up marrying her a year later.

I learned from the hometown paper that Jerry had broken his neck at the quarry when he dived into a rock in the shallow area a ways from where we had been swimming. I changed my major to philosophy that winter. Figured I'd find out if there really were true and false things in the world.

As best as I have been able to figure through my bachelor's degree in philosophy and the master's degree in psychology and twenty years of counseling folks and all that I've learned as a human being there are some things that are true and others that are false and some are both.

Wildcat
November, 1970

The security chief barged into command headquarters. "It's this simple," he said, glaring around the room at the other officers and guards. "The plant manager wants his turkeys back."

The chief was referring to the thousands of frozen birds in the Chevy dump trucks parked at the Cranston General Motors plant main gate on this day before Thanksgiving in 1970. The guards had been handing out the company gift of turkeys as the autoworkers left work that day, but then had come the wildcat strike at two p.m. The shop chairman, president, and shop committee of this local United Auto Workers union had walked through the General Motors stamping plant hitting E-stops, shutting down the presses, stopping fork lifts and tow motors, motioning for the men to follow them. By two-thirty, the parking lot was nearly empty, and the four security officers on turkey detail had been relieved of duty by eight union pickets who continued handing out the birds.

"I wished I'd had my gun," one of the young guards said.

"Yeah, if we'd had our guns we could have held the turkeys," chimed in one of the other fellows who had been on the gate.

"Just shut the fuck up," the chief said. He laid out a well-worn map and began assigning sectors to the lieutenants. The four square miles of the plant grounds were divided into six sectors, and the chief assigned one to each of the lieutenants. Both captains would be on sector one today for the assault up the hill to the main gate. Big Bill, one of the captains who had been passed over for the chief's job, rubbed his hands, each the size of a picnic ham, as he thought about kicking a little hillbilly ass on the ramp.

"Each of you," and he nodded at Big Bill, then at the other captain, "will have six men and a lieutenant. We are going up that hill, and we will take back our turkeys. The other men will secure the gate. We will move the dump trucks into the executive parking garage as soon as we take possession." He picked a dozen of the toughest out of the forty security guards. He had hired many of them, and he knew that five of the twelve were just back from Vietnam, half fucking crazy yet from their time in the bush. He would have possession of the plant manager's stupid turkeys shortly.

"We taking side arms?" asked one of the lieutenants assigned to the assault force.

"Hell no," the chief spat. "Look, you got a handful of dumbfuck hillbillies up there. They got our turkeys. We're going to take them back. You'll have your sticks and riot gear. Just push them out onto Route 30, and they can run or get run over. We'll have two snipers on the roof just in case."

Across the street at the union hall, the parking lot was full, cars spilling onto the edge of the state route running through this Ohio town that fifteen years earlier had welcomed the General Motors plant. Seen from a distance, the haphazard assemblage of vehicles looked like a junkyard, most of the pickup trucks and cars showing long, red streaks of rust. Up close, the bald tires and worn interiors were visible. These guys weren't getting rich working at GM, or if they were, they weren't spending their money on the product they made twelve hours a day, seven days a week.

Milt Jeffers, the shop chairman, leaned

back in the leather chair in his office in the new union hall and popped open another beer. He took a long swig, then sat forward and peered over his sunglasses. "What the fuck you mean, what are we going to do with the turkeys?"

"Well, I just wondered …."

"Fucking idiots, everywhere I turn," Jeffers said as he stood up and tossed his car keys to Jimmy Hatfield, his personal assistant. "Take my car over there and fill the trunk up with turkeys."

By now the second shifters had formed a single-file line on the highway as they saw the turkeys being handed out. One man in each dump truck was tossing the frozen birds, which were then handed down the line of men to the waiting cars. Crazy Jack was in charge of the operation and seemed to know all the workers, shouting to many by name as they approached to get their Thanksgiving turkeys, courtesy of General Motors and the United Auto Workers. Jack saw the chairman's Cadillac do a U-turn and swing towards the line of cars, and he stepped forward, holding his hand up to stop the next car. The chairman's boy buzzed the electric window down and popped the trunk release all at the same time. "Fill her up," he shouted, and flipped his thumb at the now open trunk.

"That goofy son of a bitch," Crazy Jack muttered and motioned to the guys to put their turkeys in the trunk. The back end of the shiny, new car was beginning to sag when Jack heard the crack of a rifle. Hell, he knew that sound, even identified it as a 30-06. He pulled his neck into his shoulders and looked around. Craaack, came another round and Jack knew that it was coming from somewhere in the parking lot of the union hall. One of the guys was shooting the video cameras off the plant walls. He shook his head and looked down the highway towards town. This was bad shit happening. Once the guns are fired, the cops show up fast.

Then Crazy Jack heard a shout. He figured the cops had already been spotted and was ready to wing it out of there. The man in the closest turkey truck gestured down the hill to the plant. About a fourth of the way up the two-hundred-yard-long concrete entrance ramp marched the assault force, shields held in front, helmets and face guards in place, sticks at the ready, just like a big city police force, with the best equipment that money could buy. They were in no hurry, marching six wide up the ramp, which was two lanes wide and skirted on the sides with 12 gauge sheet metal in place of guard rails. Big Bill called the marching cadence through his megaphone, slapping his nightstick in rhythm against his bad left leg: "Leeefft. Leeefft. Leeefft, rot, leeeeffft."

Crazy Jack came around the trucks. There were a couple dozen union guys there by now, pointing down the ramp, laughing and giving Big Bill and his boys the finger. Big Bill responded by going to a double time: "Leeft, leeft, leeft, rot, left." Here they came, GM's own private police force, going into battle for their plant manager's honor and the honor of every plant manager, every GM assistant vice-president, and the honor of the GM chairman himself.

Then there was a thunk as a turkey hit the pavement and rolled down the concrete ramp, bouncing unpredictably as only a frozen turkey can. More turkeys rolled crazily down the ramp, and then a dozen guys were on the trucks lofting frozen turkeys down the runway, turkeys careening this way and that, ricocheting off the sheet metal walls. One of the front guards went down as a turkey slammed into him.

Big Bill marched on, all his pent up resentment at his commander's incompetence and all the nepotism that ran this industry giant urging him onward and upward on the concrete ramp. He might as well have been back in Korea because he was fixing to kill somebody at the top of that damn hill when he got there. Then a turkey going about twenty miles an hour hit a rock six feet in front of him, launched itself and caught his left knee. Big Bill went down in a massive heap of beer belly, holding his left knee in pain.

And above the din of shouting and laughing and horns honking, and the thunking and banging of the frozen turkeys as they clattered and careened down the chute past the guards lying every which way, towards the plant and the reinforcement guards entering below, could be heard the wailing of sirens filling the air from every direction. The dump beds of the Chevy trucks were activated, and another two thousand frozen turkeys slid out of the beds like a flash flood toward GM's finest, and while the men all scrambled across the highway toward the union hall, the chairman's Cadillac pulled away from the scene, its rear bumper sagging from the weight of the turkeys.

Pinhead

Two weeks after leaving West Virginia, Pinhead's dad was killed on the picket line at American Rubber in Oakridge. It was Pinhead himself who had helped open the gate to allow the strikers access to the plant. One of the pickets, a friend of his dad from down home, had backed his pickup truck to the fence and attached a chain to the rear bumper hitch. All 60 pounds of the eight-year-old Pinhead was squeezed under the chain link fence with the other end of the chain, which he dragged the ten feet to the gate. In the dawn light, the guards had not seen him drop the chain loop over the slide lock on the gate. Then as Pinhead scrambled for the fence, the truck revved and tires squealed as the gate was forced open. The lock mechanism flipped into the air and sailed backwards into the group of pickets where it caught his dad in the temple.

That was the end of the strike right there. Everyone stood around the downed man waiting for the ambulance to arrive. No more rocks were thrown. The jack rocks and ball bats were tucked back into car trunks as if they were tools being put away at the end of a day's work. By the time the ambulance arrived, the plant's top management had joined the strikers in their little group and ordered the guards to fetch coffee and donuts for everyone. And then they all went inside and figured out a way to agree on a new contract.

Pinhead was thinking about that morning now as he loaded the quarter panel in the monstrous hem die. He cycled the press with the palm buttons just as the afternoon break whistle blew, and laid his oily gloves on the press bed. He looked at the pile of books he was reading right now: *Sons and Lovers, The Tin Drum*, and *The Idiot,* then grabbed the Dostoyevsky novel and started up the aisle to the break area. He had gotten the job here at the GM stamping plant through the union a year ago, just out of high school. All the union guys knew what had happened to Pinhead's dad a decade earlier and made sure the young man had a job.

Pinhead was named "Pinhead" because he always carried a stack of books with him everywhere he went. His real last name was Pinwed. After his father's death, his mother had urged all five kids to get an education–it was the only way out of poverty she could see for them. Reading became Pinhead's mission in life. His goal was to read every book in the grade school library. And he did that. In high school, he set the same goal for himself, except he was then reading fiction only, two novels a day. He would stay up late at night, take books to the bathroom or cafeteria, and carry them on his paper route after school. He was always bent over a book. His eyes became sunken with dark pouches beneath, and he was not aware of the clothes he put on each morning–he didn't know what color they were and did not notice if they were clean or dirty. As long as he had his eyes fixed on the pages, he was satisfied. He became well read, and was an expert on the novel of the nineteenth and twentieth century. Pinhead became a subject of ridicule among his schoolmates for his ever-present stack of books and his unkempt appearance.

And that was just fine with him. He grew up needing an enemy, his class warfare instincts kindled by the death of his father in the labor dispute and bolstered by the readings of Steinbeck, Lawrence, Sinclair and others. The college-bound students who were particularly bothered by Pinhead—they knew that he was better educated than them–were a good enough enemy for him. They ridiculed him on a daily basis, nicknaming him "Pinhead," tripped him in the stairwells, but stayed their distance since his only method of fighting back had become spitting.

He was accurate and more than once had ruined a preppie's day by planting a yellow mucous hocker on a Gant shirt. He would have loved to fight them and hurt them physically, but a couple years after his father's death he had nearly died of botulism. His mother's treasured pressure canner had disappeared during one of the many moves the family made from neighborhood to neighborhood in Oakridge, and she had had to rely on hot-water-bath canning for the food from her garden. The severe illness, coupled with the poor nutrition his family experienced, had left him small and weak, and physically defenseless.

Today as he clutched the paperback volume of *The Idiot*, he was stressed. The job had been a real break for him and his family. He was already eying a little bungalow in Oakridge for his mother and his younger siblings. He had money in his pocket and was going to look at a 1968 orange Camaro after work. He had spent the day thinking about the fast car, with its 396 engine and big, rear tires, and that had set him back in his reading—he should have been on track to finish *The Idiot* by bedtime tonight but was behind schedule. And then he had wondered if he would spend so much time driving the new car that he would neglect his reading. He wanted to have all of Dostoyevsky's books finished in another week and then get started on Tolstoy.

He had lately been agitated all the time. Just thinking about his mom and four siblings, and his responsibility for them, built the stress. Both his seventeen-year-old sister and sixteen-year-old brother were headed to college and he knew he was expected to help them financially, and he could do so because of this well-paid job, which he knew he was fortunate to have.

But what about him? He wanted to go to school too, but knew it would not ever be possible. He wanted some respect for the things he knew, but there was no venue in a factory for a person who was an expert on the modern novel. And having these selfish feelings made him hate himself. And hating himself was a hard thing.

He fingered his copy of *The Idiot* and held it up to look at it as he approached the break area, thinking maybe it had something to tell him. He had only read two hundred pages and the book was disconcerting to him because he was an idiot, too. He was a "Pinhead" and never knew how to act about anything.

When he was waiting for the machine to fill his paper cup with the foamy, watered-down coffee, he heard it: "Pinhead." He looked around to see who had said it. He thought that once out of high school no one would know that he was Pinhead. He had not been called Pinhead since he had hired in to the GM plant. But there sat one of his preppy ex classmates. "Hey, Pinhead," the other called, not in an unfriendly manner, but Pinhead reacted. His stress and resulting mental state had crippled his emotions.

He turned and almost spat, and imagined the spit wad floating across the break area and settling onto the t-shirt of the other young man. Ah Jeez, Pinhead said to himself as he backed from the break area, leaving his coffee in the machine, clutching his book tightly to his chest. He walked slowly back to his job, opened his dad's old black metal lunch bucket for the cookies his mother had packed, glanced at the paperwork from the realtor—his mother would love the house—sat down on the metal stool, opened *The Idiot*, and began reading.

JIM

Jim twisted the skinny trunk of his body in a fast, violent jerk just as the cop grabbed the buckle of his left Harley Davidson boot. When the boot flopped off, Jim found himself sitting upright, ready to jump up and run. But then he felt the baton lock down on his neck. He started to fight it off, but the other cop stomped on his bare ankle and the struggle was over.

He looked for his three grandkids through cold drizzle. It was November, the last game of the year for his eighth grader grandson, and he had volunteered to take the three younger grandkids to the game. No one had told him it would cost $13 for the four of them to get in–$3 each for the kids and $4 for him. He didn't have $13.

So he had told that to the young lady collecting the money. "I'm sorry. I don't have any money." The kids had already scampered ahead and there was nothing he thought he could do.

As he lay on the cinder track that circled the football field, he glimpsed Sissy playing alongside the wooden bleachers. That made him happy even with the heavy man standing on his ankle. "Come on, Jim. Put your other hand back here."

Jim pictured the puzzled look on the face of the money-taker at the gate. She never said a word, just flipped her right wrist up a couple of times while he shrugged and sidled after the kids. He never thought it would be a crime not to have any money for the after-school football game.

Jim had never changed his hair style since he had first slicked it into a ducktail in 1958, and now the hair held bits of cinders and leaves where he had fallen when taken down. He wanted to ask for sympathy, tell this son of the cop who had first busted him over 40 years ago that it would kill him to go back to prison for violating his probation, which is what he was doing the moment he refused to walk back to the gate with the cops.

"Damn, Jim," the cop said, and wrenched the plastic tie tighter. "You never learn."

Sitting up again, Jim watched the kids near him on the track. "Grandpa! Can I get hot chocolate?" called the boy. "And a hot dog," Sissy chimed in.

Jim looked around the stadium, not changed much from 1959, when he had scored eight touchdowns in his first three games as a ninth grader before being kicked off the team for smoking in the alley beside the teacher parking lot. Ah, shit. If he hadn't smoked, hadn't got drunk so many times, hadn't stole some chicken shit motorcycle parts and gotten caught up in the system.

Jim heard the cheering and turned to watch his lanky young grandson outrunning the entire field to score another touchdown, and a tear rolled down his fresh-shaven cheek. He could feel it moving slowly, like it might never get where it was going.

The Rogue

The Blazer had been in the workshop garage for a week when Jody found it.

A massive, red creature with rust holes and missing wheel wells, it reminded her of the cars Tim drove when he had worked for the junkyard the first year they were married. She laughed–another project.

There was the old Lyman he had bought for $300. Two years he spent patching dry-rotted sections, fitting the new mahogany transom, and rebuilding the V-8 Gray Marine engine. The '51 Ford Pickup he had brought back to life. But this new decayed beast? No way.

After Tim had wheel barrowed the firewood to the house after work, and carried it in, Jody cornered him about the Blazer.

"Just an idea," he told her. "Earl at work, I've told you about him, was going to junk the thing. It's 15 years old but only has 60,000 miles on it."

After supper, Tim was in his shop. When Jody left to pick her sister up at work, she looked in on him. The air compressor was going full and Tim was slicing off body panels with a cutting wheel.

Every night after his chores he went to the workshop. When he had exposed the areas needed, he began fitting angle iron braces the full length of the body and across the back. As he welded the passenger side he realized that the door would never open again. No need–there would not be a passenger.

When the angle iron work was complete, Tim told Jody not to mention that he was working on the Blazer.

"Why? Everyone knows when you're working on something."

"Not this time. I'm not sure what I'm going to do with it. Just don't tell anybody about it." It sounded like an order, which Tim did not often give. But she laughed. He used to drink way too much, stopping off with the guys after work as often as he came home. The summer he built the workshop had put an end to his drinking. "Of course I won't tell anybody." She imagined that the vehicle was to be a surprise for someone.

Through the fall he cut and riveted body panels to the Blazer contour, covering over the angle iron armor. By Christmas the entire body was glazed to perfection and coated with burgundy enamel so deep it appeared black except in sunshine.

The motor had been in his buddy's machine shop. He had kept the 350 block and worked it up to 300 horsepower. That should give him all the power he needed.

While the engine was being re-worked, Tim inspected all of the underbody and drive train. He changed all the fluids, examined the transfer cases, and put in all new U-joints. Everything was in perfect condition. Then he fitted the four-inch thick, 16-inch-wide oak bumper he had had cut at an Amish sawmill. The Rogue was finished.

The General Motors stamping plant where he worked was on a ten-hour, seven-day-a-week operation again. For 30 straight days he worked, finally taking a day off only for Jody's birthday. Over dinner at the small steak-house-tavern they both loved, Jody asked what he was going to do with his "perfect" Blazer.

"I don't know," he told her. "It was just something else to keep me out of trouble, I guess." He couldn't tell her, not anyone. If he went ahead with his plan, no one could know about it.

The other die makers at work were all fired up the day after the plant closing was officially announced. They had known for nearly a year, but hadn't felt the reality of the closing. Normally conservative, they now bordered on lunacy. "Let's get all the ex-Navy people in the UAW together, buy a submarine and sink the Jap cars on the way here!"

"Nah," said another. "Let's have a ball peen hammer party. Give me ten good men, and I'll trash a whole car lot of foreign cars in 20 seconds. You just run through, dent all the body panels, break lots of windows and they're out of business."

"Felony charge," said Don, the lawyer of the group. "Jail time if you get caught."

"What do you think we should do, peace-breath?" asked Joe, the lead man on the shift.

"Write letters," Don said. "Congressmen. Senators."

Everyone laughed.

As Tim set about mixing the epoxy to pass the trim from the master, he decided the time was right. The guys would only talk – not buy a sub, ball peen Toyotas, or write letters. They would grouse, watch the calendar, and haul their 20- or 30-year accumulation of tools and skills to the unemployment line.

Tim shut out all these thoughts. The master adapter, an outer door, was waxed, the epoxy ready and the upper and lower trim steels within an eighth of an inch. An apprentice stood watching as Tim began packing the epoxy onto the trim steels.

He worked for a half hour, the apprentice learning a skill central to die making. By two o'clock the job was finished, Tim washed up, and got a coffee.

The Blazer had never been registered for plates. No reason to put plates on the Rogue. After work he gassed it up from five-gallon cans until the gauge read full. He started the engine and let the machine warm up. Its throaty power shook the garage door. He turned off the machine and locked in the four-wheel drive.

It was eleven p.m. when he slipped out of bed without waking Jody. In the laundry room, he slipped on the black sweat suit he had hidden there earlier. Then he was in the workshop. He backed the Blazer out and was on his way.

The destination was two blocks away, a Yuppie bar that charged just enough for drinks to keep out the riff-raff.

He parked far back in the parking lot and waited. An Olds Cierra pulled out, followed ten minutes later by a Cavalier wagon. Then a Saab started up. Tim started the Blazer's engine, the adrenalin pumping, but he let it go. Swedish cars weren't the problem. He might even buy one if it weren't for the greedy Japanese ruining the market for all foreign makes.

After another ten minutes, a Toyota Camry pulled out of the parking lot. Tim kept a good distance behind until they were to the stop light by the freeway. At the instant the light turned green, Tim was inches away from the Toyota. He engaged the Blazer's bumper with the tinny Japanese bumper.

Tim punched the accelerator to the floor, squealing all four tires and the car in front of him took off. The driver, after going several frantic yards, pushed his brakes but it did no good. The Toyota's little tires and brakes screeched and squealed. Tim let off as the Toyota careened off the freeway and into the grassy median.

Home, Tim slipped back into bed. Jody turned and muttered something in her sleep and slid close to him. He lay for some time, feeling her warmth and savoring his success–at least he had acted–done something. His job would be gone. In a year he would likely lose his home and have to move away from his home town.

Next morning at work his buddies were huddled together with their coffee, passing the morning paper around, laughing and carrying on. The paper was passed to Tim and he read the police report. A motorist reported that a crazy semi-truck driver had pushed his Toyota for half a mile. No damage had been reported to the Toyota, but the story had seemed zany enough to make the front page. Local police were puzzled, the report said.

He laughed, passed the paper on, finished his coffee, and got to work. The trim steels had all been taken off the die shoe, meaning that his work the day before had been successful. He felt proud that he had completed a major step on the die he had been building for five months. If the epoxy hadn't taken or had smudged the trim line, he would have had to do it over again.

He worked hard all day, profiling the hardened steels to match them to the smooth epoxy edge. After work he was tired, stopping in the parking lot to snort steel and epoxy dust into his handkerchief.

He didn't know where he would hit tonight. While he hauled wood he thought about it – another Yuppie bar – maybe the one where his ex-friend Tom hung out. A Mazda. Tom had bought a Mazda RX-7.

Tim pictured Tom squealing the thing up his driveway for a cookout, jumping out and asking Tim to take a look at it.

Tim had been amazed. He thought he knew his old friend. He had thought hard, wondering what he should do, why his friend had bought a foreign car.

"Get it out of here."

Tom was perplexed. "What do you mean?" he asked.

"Move it, the junk, or I'll take a sledge hammer to it."

No more words were spoken. Tim screeched his Jap machine down the road and that was the end of it. Never saw each other again.

After supper, just at dark, Jody went to the grocery. In minutes, Tim had the Blazer on the road. He headed for the mall a couple of miles away.

When he got there he stopped at the edge of the parking lot. Thousands of cars, the mall lights reflecting off their shiny tops.

Tim sat thinking. What the hell was he doing? Committing a criminal act for what? The plant would be closed, he and his co-workers would be thrust into a world without decent jobs, and many of them would see their dreams disappear–college for their children or grandchildren, the Lake Erie boat for retirement, or travel they had dreamed of all their working years.

Tim thought about his attempts to buy American-made products at this very mall last Christmas. Not much available. Clerks looked at him like he was crazy when he asked where the American-made shirts were.

He put the Blazer in gear and drove through the lot. If the government had only done something …. If fair trade had been sought by Reagan …. If folks bought American products ….

A box-like vehicle pulled out in front of Tim. He braked and then recognized it as an Isuzu Trooper. General Motors actually owned part of the company that made the junk in front of him and now General Motors was shutting down his plant.

On the expressway, Tim pulled smoothly into contact with the Isuzu. The 350 engine blasted into action. Ahead of him Tim watched the hysterical driver, who looked from the mirror to the speedometer, shifted gears and applied the brakes. But the inferior metal in front of the Blazer had no chance.

As Tim hit 60 he slammed on the brakes. The Isuzu, out of control, veered into the ditch and turned over. Tim wheeled the Blazer into a U-turn and crossed the median.

Every night Tim managed to trash a least one foreign car–A BMW, Toyotas, Mazdas and a Yugo, which slid like a match box before the Blazer.

But he took no satisfaction from what he was doing. He was now a criminal. He had caused tens of thousands of dollars of damage to cars belonging to the citizens of his community.

The newspaper continued to carry stories of his exploits, labeling him the "mystery truck." No one could identify the make or color of the vehicle. When Tim acted, it all happened fast. The newspaper reports promised swift prosecution by the police chief and sheriff.

Jody finally put it all together. One day when Tim got home, he found her inspecting the scarred oak bumper on the Rogue.

"Welcome home, mystery truck," she said.

"Somebody had to do it," he said.

"Do what? Go to prison?"

He sidled over to the work bench and picked up a bearing, handling it like a jeweler with a watch.

She watched for a few moments. This talented and wonderful man. She would lose him if he were caught. "You!" she shouted.

Jody walked over to him, and he examined the bearing. "It's junk," he said, threw it into the scrap barrel in the corner, and turned to face her.

She hugged him, and tears were dripping down her cheeks. "You can't do this, Timmy."

"I had to do something."

Now she was crying big tears. He didn't want to fight with her. When she recovered, Jody said, "You can't. You're so smart. You'll get another job. You're good at what you do. You'll find something right away. You could make a living right here in your workshop." She was talking fast, hyper. She was always like that when she was beside herself over something Tim was doing that was stupid.

He squeegeed the tears down her cheeks with his forefingers.

"Yeah, I'll make it. But not all the others. We're a family at work. If a guy is trying, and gets into trouble, we all bail him out."

She shook her head. "What's that got to do with being a criminal?"

Tim shrugged. He knew the answer was "nothing." "I'll quit after tonight," he said.

She rushed out of the workshop and to the house. He didn't follow, just waited for the early winter darkness and tinkered with the Rogue.

Then he was on his way. Just a couple of miles and one more foreign car and he would quit. Tim waited once he spotted Tom's Toyota Corolla. He got angry when he remembered the good times he and Tom used to have. Why did he have to buy a foreign car?

At 7:30 Tom and a couple of friends came out of the Yuppie tavern. By the time Tom had said his good byes and gotten into his car, Tim and the Rogue were ready.

A couple hundred yards out of the parking lot Tim hooked up with the tiny car in front of him. He was still angry and hit it hard. The Rogue blasted the little car along and then the Toyota went off the road and hit a telephone pole.

Tim did a U-turn. He was ready to punch it down and make his last getaway when he realized that Tom might be hurt.

But when he had parked and walked over to the Mazda, Tom was grinning at him out the window. "It's you! I thought maybe you were the one."

"Are you all right?"

"Yeah. But you sure screwed my car up."

Tim looked at the damage. "I think it's totaled," Tom was grinning. "You gonna turn me in?" Tim asked.

Tom laughed. "Actually you did me a favor. The transmission's shot. Would have cost me a couple of grand to fix it."

The Rogue sat idling a few yards away. "That thing for sale?" Tom asked.

"If I get home."

"Then get it home. I'll stop over in a couple of days …. How much?"

Tim got in the Rogue and called, "It's yours if you want it."

The paper the next day showed a picture of the crumpled Toyota with Tom explaining that a candy-apple Kenworth cab-over had rear-ended him.

Tim ignored all the fuss at work over the newspaper report. He was done with it, and he was building the last die he would ever build for General Motors. He would stamp his name on this one, on the upper shoe where all the specs were stamped–the shut height, part number, weight, etc. This would be the best die ever built in the world, no modifications needed before production, and it would have his name stamped on it.

Portrait of a Robot

He doesn't know how he got this way. Crazy, that is. Most things, you think about them long enough, you come up with an answer. All he knows for sure is that he got to work this morning in his Chevy pickup, the laundry is done, there are ham sandwiches in his lunch pail, and that next Saturday he gets to see his kids.

The draw die booms at the front of the line and he switches on the conveyor. Panels come, and it's load, hit the buttons, load, hit the buttons.

It seems noisier than usual this morning. They've turned everything up a notch again. Air hisses like angry snakes at his feet, scrap clatters down the chutes, the floor vibrates: squealing, clanging, grinding, scraping, shearing, the hundreds of presses going to war.

He reaches for the palm buttons and a tremendous explosion brings him off his feet. He starts shaking, can't help it, and turns off the conveyor. A 40-ton die has just been dropped by a crane twenty feet from him.

Could get squashed like a bug in here, like old Hendricks on the door line, got his head caught in a welder. Said it was suicide ... Ha! ... something spooked him and he fell in.

Then he sees the foreman charging along the press line. The boss don't scare this guy any. "Get me the safety man!"

"Turn that conveyor on." The boss's eyes are bloodshot from his nightly drunk.

He feels his shoulder twitch. No. Hitting him again might get him fired. Felt good the time he floored him, though. The boss looks up to the ceiling and acts real sad, like maybe he's got problems, too. "What's the deal?"

He points to the die. "Get the line going and I'll call safety."

He thinks of Granddad's farm for some reason. When they lived in that coal camp he used to hike back to the home place to see Gramps. If only the old man could be here. He'd know what to do with this place–maybe plow it under and start over.

"Get the conveyor on." He feels his shoulder twitch again and it scares him. Boss takes him upstairs, he'll get time off, just get behind in child support.

The foreman shakes his head and walks away. Guess he don't need trouble either. He turns on his belt and loads the panels, hits the buttons, sinks into the rhythm.

At break he heads up to the locker room with Al. He downs most of the Coke he bought at the vending area. Al grins and fills their cups from his bottle of Jim Beam. Al was in his division in Korea. Never knew him there, but it's a sort of kinship – that and the fact they grew up not ten miles from each other in Southern West Virginia.

They sit watching the black smoke curl out of the stack at the powerhouse. The drink goes down easy. "Couple them kids went home already. Double time and all they can think about is getting out of here."

He shakes his head. "Never been hungry, I guess." Double time, though? That's right! Today *is* Sunday.

Al laughs. "Little brats don't know what work is. Like to get 'em out in the fields for a day."

Al pours himself another one and holds the bottle out. "I'm good," he says and in a minute they ride the escalator down to the pressroom. As they split up he thinks about what Al said about working the fields. He never minded that, even the tobacco cutting. Come to think of it, those days sort of shine out from all the rest of his life.

He sets his drink on the greasy die shoe and pictures Granddad, Uncle John, Dad and him and the other kids out there. It was always sweet and damp in the morning. They'd be hot by noon, sweating and hungry, but there would be lunch of beans and taters and cornbread. Good thing, in a way, Korea came along and he got out of there before he went in the mines.

The drink eases the morning along, and the noise can't get to him; but the building's vibrating now. He always wonders why it don't fall down.

He wishes he knew how he got this way. Depressive neurosis, the doctor always calls it. This time he's going to make it, though. Got the best job anybody'd want. Made good money the last couple of years when he wasn't sick. He was going to quit, but the doc talked him out of it.

Wishes he was still married. But it don't do a bit of good to think back all them years to how it was. It's him being crazy that did it. She and the kids just moved out one day while he was at work. All he ever done was try to make a living.

The doc figured it was from Korea, some sort of delayed reactive neurosis. Guess so, but he is never able to come up with anything real bad that happened there. All he remembers from the last few months of being married is he was real tired and fell asleep in his chair every night.

Well, least he can retire in 12 more years. You work hard, you get what's coming to you. Don't know what he'll do all day, though. Don't do nothing now when he has a day off.

The lunch whistle blows and he shuts down the conveyor and press. All there is now is this loud hum from all the 440 electric motors winding down. He checks the meter–only eleven hundred more panels and they're finished. He grabs his lunch pail, buys a Coke, and heads upstairs to the locker room.

He'll call the kids on the phone when he gets home today–that's what he'll do–make sure Tom's keeping his grades up at Ohio State. Ain't everybody can afford to send their kids to college. He hopes Tom knows that.

Public Relations

Darius Delaney got the call at 4:30 p.m. on Sunday, a half hour after he had gotten home from guard drill. The call meant he would have to leave immediately for Cranston, Ohio, to quell another labor disturbance at a plant that had been jamming the GM parts pipeline for the past 10 years. "Enough is enough," he was told by the GM president, who was in the Bahamas for the holidays. "Take care of it."

Darius was the first special assistant to the president of General Motors. He was a fireman in the Michigan National Guard. He was an MBA graduate of the School of Business at Miami University. He was a member of the prestigious Phiwi fraternity, which was famous nationwide, no, worldwide, for its luau every fall on the Oxford, Ohio, campus. And Darius had served as the chairman of the luau for three consecutive years during his time at Miami, a period of service unmatched ever by any other fraternity brother.

The luau was not trusted to just anyone;

rather, there were usually enough complaints every year–the Tri Delt freshmen wore panties to the party, the pig was done too late, or maybe the baby oil ran out at midnight–always some detail that caused enough grumbling to ensure a yearly turnover of chairmen. But Darius had proven himself three times, and only finally relinquished the position because it was time for him to move on–"Time to grow up, boy"–as his grandfather and GM vice-president of sales pronounced, "and come put the GM yoke around your neck and get ready to be somebody."

The same day Grandpa had arranged his National Guard physical, Darius had interviewed for his first GM position. He and Grandpa never dreamed that he would be starting out in the president's office. In fact, the old man had laughed, if he had known that, the National Guard thing would not have been necessary–Darius would have been exempt from the draft by virtue of his high position in a company so necessary to the national defense of the United States of America.

What had landed Darius this advanced starting position was none other than the fact that he had been chairman of the Phiwi luau for three consecutive years. As a past president of the

Phiwi chapter at Duke, the corporate personnel director had been privy to a permanent invitation to the yearly bash, though finally one year at age 25, when he awoke in the kitchen naked with a pair of men's underwear around his neck, he never went back again. But he knew, as did anyone who knew about such things, that a man who could be trusted to be in charge of the Phiwi luau for three years could be trusted with anything GM had to throw at him.

So it was that Darius Delaney found himself on Route 23 near Carey, Ohio, on November 29, 1970, at 8:00 p.m. He had hustled in to GM headquarters where he had been met by the president's secretary and briefed on the Cranston situation. He needed to leave immediately, he had been informed. This was bad news to Darius since he and his fiancée had planned an evening together once he was back in town from guard duty. He had hinted over the phone from the base that he was horny, and Melanie had admitted the same, and for a nice girl like Melanie to say she was horny meant that Darius had a pleasurable evening before him.

But now, surrounded by the corn stubble of dark Ohio farmland, Darius was not going to get laid. He was going to get a hotel room that smelled like old shoes in a town full of fucking hillbillies whose main goal in life seemed to be to fuck up the works of the largest corporation in the world. And he was going to put a stop to it.

The United Auto Workers Union was a pain in Darius Delaney's ass. If not for the union, it would be smooth sailing for the company–record profits every year instead of a struggle to match last year's. And without the UAW, Darius would have smooth career advancement. The recent national strike, which started on September 14 and lasted sixty-seven days, had left him exhausted. He had been on the go the entire time, writing press releases, flying here and there to offer his superb organizational skills wherever they were needed. And yet the union had kicked the company's ass. Thirty years and out for retirement. That meant a man could possibly retire at age forty-eight with a monthly income of $400! That wasn't right in Darius' mind. That and the wage increases would cause inflation. And dental care? That was unheard of for any industry, yet the UAW had gotten it for all the hillbillies and their families. More money, cost of living wage increases, more holidays, more health insurance, retirement. It might not have seemed so bad to him, but he was sitting at the bargaining table as it happened. He wasn't responsible for the negotiating and the giving in, but he was sure that anyone who was a party to this boondoggle of a contract would go nowhere within the giant company in the future. Only a bunch of losers would have agreed to such a contract. And Darius Delaney wasn't a loser. He had chaired three consecutive Phiwi luaus!

By the time he reached the edge of Cranston, Darius had hatched a plan. He would design an ad for the local newspaper blaming the United Auto Workers for the deaths at the plant, saying that the hourly workers who died had been killed for not supporting the union. That's what he would do. He would make a name for himself on this strike. It was this local UAW union in Cranston that had caused more trouble than any other local union in the country. It was this bunch of hillbillies that was the enemy. Darius Delaney would bring the UAW to its fucking knees!

Darius had to pass the plant to get to his hotel in downtown Cranston, and was shocked at what he saw. At all three gates on Route 30, there were huge bonfires, each with at least a dozen men sitting around drinking beer. Others stood along the highway, holding their picket signs aloft for the entire world to see that they were in charge of this General Motors plant. Darius was pissed.

As soon as he checked into the Imperial Hotel, he called the city police. He wanted action now, but the dispatcher on duty at the tail end of this holiday weekend told him he would have to come down to the station and file charges. He slammed the phone down and then dialed the sheriff's department number. He got a similar response to his call for the cavalry to come swooping down on the hillbillies and throw them off his property. "Yes, I own the fucking property," he found himself shouting into the phone at the dispatcher. "I am management! I own it!"

It just happened that Sheriff Thomas Greene was at the office making sure his orders to make an hourly check of the plant were being carried out. He was concerned over the fatalities even though his initial investigations had shown that all but one appeared to be accidental. He was on his way through the dispatcher's office when he heard the shouting over the phone receiver, which he took from the bewildered young woman at the desk. "You will do what I tell you to do!" Darius shouted.

"Who is this?" Thomas asked.

"This is General Motors! Who is this?" Darius shouted.

"Sheriff Greene here."

"Ahhhh. About time. Now here is what you are going to do," Darius said.

Thomas chuckled as he heard the usual GM tantrum begin. "And what would that be?"

"Why, for starters, enforce the law. There are too many pickets."

Thomas shook his head. He had made sure that no vandalism was taking place by having his deputies drive past the plant every hour. If they knew the pickets, the deputies were free to stop and talk in order to get more information for the sheriff. He was concerned this time. The men had just completed a sixty-seven-day strike and had only worked three days when they went on the first wildcat. That one was just for fun compared to this one. The shop chairman and the president were both fired, leaving no local leadership in the union. And both of them were popular leaders. If it had not been a holiday weekend, the sheriff would have been in contact with GM and UAW brass in Detroit to get things moving. The United Auto

Workers International Union had grown just as weary of the Cranston plant as had General Motors. Thomas Greene was worried about real violence if this thing did not get settled. He knew many of the men at the plant and knew what they were capable of.

"Do you understand me, sir?" Darius barked at the sheriff.

"Yes sir," Thomas answered, thinking ahead to tomorrow when he could get some assistance from Detroit. Whoever this pissant on the phone was, it wouldn't do any good to get him more fired up than he already was.

Darius set to work on his ad. "Five men are dead because of the United Auto Workers," it would read in bold print. "Just when you think the union can stoop no lower, it resorts to murder," the ad would read in fine print. Darius stared at his document. Maybe that was a bit much, he thought, but knew he needed to get *some* kind of information in the paper tomorrow. GM was already losing the public relations battle, witness the morning's *Cranston Journal*. He had looked at the front-page story, "Five Dead at Local GM Plant." The first couple of paragraphs covered the deaths of the five men. The third one was what had caught Darius' attention.

> After a 67 day national strike to secure basic cost of living wage increases and a decent retirement, the local United Auto Workers union has seen the need to once again strike the local GM stamping plant. The difference between all the other strikes and this one is the obvious anger among the rank and file.

Darius had planned to get the ad out in the morning, but after reading the newspaper story decided to take it downtown tonight. Quick action was needed.

Editor Tom Finnegan was still at his desk late Sunday night. He was convinced he knew what had happened at the GM plant. And it wasn't just a one-day occurrence that had resulted in five more deaths at the factory, but a cumulative, abstract sort of cancer that was festering out there and destroying lives and families. He wasn't sure that he should write the truth, indeed, that he *could* write the truth. First, he had to be vigilant that his feelings about what had happened to Bobby stayed under control. In addition, he knew that the following days would bring the GM Public Relations brass into town, and also that the owners of the paper would be interested in what he had to say before this thing was finished. And just then his phone rang. It was the shift editor. GM had just dropped off an ad for the morning paper. And he was a little concerned over it. "Bring it up," Tom said.

All it took was for Tom Finnegan to read the GM ad and he proceeded with his editorial:

> The deaths Saturday, November 28, 1970, at the local General Motors stamping plant are a continuation of the irresponsible behavior of General Motors to the community of Cranston. The tragedy on that day brings to ten the total number of men who have died within the walls of that plant in as many years, leaving children, and parents and wives and brothers and sisters to grieve at the unnecessary losses of life.
>
> It appears that GM's

arrogance in handling personnel matters is out of control as this time the plant fired the union's leadership. Firing these men is the equivalent of the union kidnapping and holding for ransom the plant manager of the local plant. GM has been asking for trouble, and it appears that this time they have gotten it.

Back in his room, Darius stared at the wall. "Bring 'em to their fucking knees," he said to himself. He drank three beers and each time he popped a can he said it again.

Hill Tide

As Vienna jostled among the church crowd and exchanged greetings she tried to recall the sound of the spring that spurted year round from the base of the hill behind the cabin at the farm. But the voices and the heat prevented her from hearing anything but a dull humming noise as if everything around her were vibrating. She was at the door shaking the minister's hand.

"Glad to see you, Mrs. Taylor. You're looking well."

"Thank you," she answered, and wondered, as she was enveloped by the sweltering heat outside, how she had come to be where she was at this very moment.

She walked slowly. A group of children played in a lot behind the Gulf station on the corner. Decisions had shaped her path, caused her to be out this afternoon on a busy street in South Charleston that went for miles past warehouses and factories, and led finally into the hills, where she knew the smoky haze of the valley would be left behind. But everyone made decisions.

She continued on her way, deep in thought. She was a thinker; the years of isolation in her big house had, if nothing else, caused her to spend many hours and days thinking. But more often than not she felt as if she were in a maze, and that thinking only led her deeper into it. So it was now as she thought of her life. And what her mind told her, what it showed her about her life, was not much: only that every thought she ever had and that every decision she ever made had placed her, at this very moment, on this dingy street in the midst of the stinking chemical factories of Charleston, West Virginia.

Then she was at the door of the big, white house. It was too large for her to take care of anymore. Once it had served a purpose, providing the room for her four children, who were now pursuing their own lives. One of them, the oldest, had become a doctor; another was an engineer. But they had all but forgotten her. The letters came seldom, if ever, and the visits had stopped long ago.

As she opened the heavy, wooden door and entered the old house, her thoughts were of the farm and the joy she had felt as a child growing up there. She ate, and after sitting for an hour or so, mentally exploring what she could remember of her childhood, called her sister.

"Hello, Myrna. How are you?"

"Oh, I'm fine. But it's so hot."

"I was thinking … I'm going for a ride to cool off. Would you like to come?"

"What a grand idea."

"Okay, I'll pick you up."

She grew excited as she drove to Myrna's. At least, she thought, she was breaking the monotony of her routine, that sameness that made up her days. As she wheeled the old Chrysler through the familiar streets she pictured her wiry, mustached father riding the plow along behind the horses.

Myrna was waiting on the porch. When she was in the car she suggested, "Let's drive up to Cane Creek and see the Johnson's."

"No," Vienna answered quickly, "Let's go down to the river."

"What river? The Coal or Kanawha?"

"No. Our river."

Myrna looked confused. "You mean down to the farm?" she exclaimed. "I don't think so…you know what Daddy said before he died.

He said never go near there. It's all grown up and there never was a road built past the farm."

"Yes. That's *our* river. Wouldn't you love to see it again?"

Myrna was silent as they started the ascent into the hills. At one curve a goat sat on a rock ledge overlooking the road. She was glad they were in the country and besides she knew she couldn't change Vienna's mind once it was made up. "Okay," she finally said. "I'll go, but only because … because I want you to see how foolish you are, always talking about that desolate, old farm."

Vienna liked to see the cabins along the creeks, the saw mills, and the people. She even liked the dingy, skeleton-like remains of the coal mines – at least they reminded her of things she had known when she was young. The city had no childhood memories to give her, she thought, envying the people who sat on their porches in the shade of huge trees and who had mountains for back yards.

All afternoon they drove through small towns, coming closer to the farm their father had homesteaded after the Civil War. In the distance, Vienna saw a string of engines laboring their way out of the hills with a line of coal cars trailing behind and a memory flashed: *She and Myrna and Perry had just come down the wagon trail on their way to school. They had to wait for the train to go past on its way to the next siding, which was near the school. Perry ran alongside one of the cars, and jumped for the ladder, intending to ride to school. But he slipped as his foot hit the frost-covered rung and almost didn't hang on. After he had recovered from the near fall, laughter took the place of his fright, and clowning, Perry hung from the ladder with one hand to show his sisters he wasn't at all scared. Then came the jolt. Perry fell and the car skidded along the slick rails, severing his legs. He writhed on the gravel for a few moments before he lost consciousness, and when Vienna reached him, his blood-spurting stumps were covered with cinders. "Get Mamma!" she cried to Myrna who stood in tears where she had been when Perry fell.*

"Look out!" Myrna cried as car veered into their lane on a curve. Vienna jerked the wheel to the right and barely missed it. When they were on a straight stretch of road, Myrna said, "Let's turn back."

"Turn back! Why, we're almost there." She had to see the farm now, if only for a moment. She had to see the spot where Perry had died in her arms. She had to see things as they had been.

Vienna drove several miles south along the Tug River until they came to the bridge to Kentucky. There she stopped at a combination gas station and church. "Hello," she said to the man who came out. "Can you tell me the best way to Larson Creek?"

He looked to his feet and stirred the gravel with first one foot and then the other. Brushing his matted hair back, he squinted into the car. "What business y'all got there?"

"We used to live there. How long have you lived here?"

"Not long."

"Oh," she said, and since he had nothing of the past to share with her, asked again about the way.

"You kin go a ways down the Kentucky side," he said pointing to the bridge, "and walk the river on the foot bridge. Or you kin go behind the place here and take the railroad utility road."

She thanked him, and they started along the cinder road beside the railroad. Shacks lined the bank. Many of the buildings were deserted.

In the inhabited ones, families sat on the lopsided porches watching Vienna's Chrysler intently. Barefoot children ran along behind in the dust until they were shouted back. Vienna stopped at a shack that had a "Barber Shop" sign on it. Two men sat on the porch drinking beer. She got out of the car to ask directions and the men walked out to her. She looked at the taller of the two. "What's your name?" she blurted.

"Oapie."

"Oapie ... Oapie Watson!" He looked surprised.

"I'm Vienna Taylor ... Don't you remember me?"

He stretched his neck forward. "It's been a long while, ain't it?"

"It's been so long I don't even recognize much here," she said looking around. "We're looking for Steepgut Creek. As I remember, it should be right around here."

"About fifty yards further. You can't see it. It's all growed over." He pointed down the tracks. "Right where that big tree limb sticks out of the growth. That's where Larson Creek goes under the railroad." The other man went back to the porch where he carefully placed his empty bottle in the top beer case.

"Does anybody still live up the creek where our place was?"

"No, ain't nobody been up there for years."

"Well, we're going up and look around," Vienna said, and turned to Myrna, who sat looking straight ahead. "You remember Oapie here, don't you? Imagine, after all these years, Oapie's still here!" Myrna sat still, her lips drawn tight.

Oapie stepped forward as Vienna turned to get in the car. "You don't want to go up there. Snakes all over the place."

"I used to live there. You can't scare me with your snake stories."

"Ain't wanting to scare you. But the strip mine does it–they stir up the snakes and they come down here. I kilt one right here under the porch t'other day."

"Well, I'll take my chances," she said, getting into the car. "Thank you, Oapie," she called as she drove away.

"Let's leave, Vienna," Myrna said. "I'm scared of these people. They aren't our kind anymore."

"Nonsense."

Myrna looked back. The other man had joined Oapie at the road where they stood staring after the car. "What are they staring at, then?"

Vienna parked the car in front of an abandoned shack and grabbed her cane off the back seat. "Are you coming?" she asked as she got out of the car.

"No, I don't want to see it."

She picked her way up the railroad bed, crossed the tracks, and stood looking down the eroded bank of the creek. The water was muddy with traces of orange running through it. Trees grew on the wagon road her father had cleared. She looked ahead to the hill, before which would stand the cabin. At the top were great bare spots, and scattered down the hillside were huge rocks and piles of debris. Briar patches, stunted trees, and weeds covered the fields her father had farmed. After a couple more minutes she could see the chimney, which she found was the only part of the cabin still standing.

She heard a train whistle in the distance and stopped. The river was visible below. A junked car protruded from a shallow spot. There was a graveyard on the far bank. A fire had destroyed the cabin. The barn still stood, but most of the siding had rotted away. She had expected to find things much as she had left them, but saw now that time had done its work.

Then she saw the spring and started towards it to get a drink. She stepped over a charred log and felt something sharp tear at her leg. She thought it was a briar or a piece of barbed wire, but then she saw the copperhead. Drops of blood oozed out the tiny holes in her calf. She flung the snake away with the cane and went on to the spring. After a long drink she started back.

She wasn't worried that she had been bitten; it wasn't her first snake bite. But she felt dizzy after a few steps. She sat down on a flat rock between the spring and the chimney. Feeling very tired, she lay down on the grass, aware of the spoilage and waste that lay all around. Yet she was glad to be here, and for the first time in many years, felt at peace. As she lost consciousness she was a girl of ten helping her father feed the animals late on a summer evening, and the cool breeze that had picked up at the coming of dusk was welcome after the heat of the day.

Myrna had started to follow Vienna, but turned back before she had gone far. The train had come and she had stood at the bottom of the wagon road waiting for it to pass. As the heavy carriages rumbled by, she remembered Vienna screaming, "Get Mamma!"

Myrna made her way back to the car. She watched for Vienna to return along the creek bank until it was too dark to see anything. As night sounds and evening mist surrounded the car, Myrna began crying softly. She felt the cool air blowing down from the mountain and smelled wood smoke, and wondered how she had come to be where she was at this very moment.

The Artificial Dick

I took the package from the mailman and rushed inside to see what I had bought.

It was that hot, still night a week ago when I ordered it. Right at 3:00 A.M. I got tired of tossing in the soggy bed so I got up and turned on the TV in the living room. I scanned through the channels, seeing mostly advertisements for jewelry and tummy-flattening machines until I clicked past a woman waving a plastic penis in the air. I clicked back to the channel and there were two girls talking about the artificial cock.

"Great penetration … a full eight inches … see how it flexes?"

Not to be outdone, the other girl reached under the counter and pulled out this massive cock and flopped it back and forth. She looked kind of like Mary Alice's daughter from church, and I wondered at the time what had ever become of that girl. Mary Alice always bragged about her being in television and someday the movies, but I had never seen her on anything till then, maybe.

I set the package on the kitchen table where the grandkids were coloring the backs of used copy-machine paper Susie brought home from the technical college. One corner of the package was all mussed up like it had been pulled back. What if the mailman had opened it and looked? My hands shook as I washed the last couple of cereal bowls and set them on the drainer.

Out the window over the sink I watched our dog, a reddish-colored mongrel, digging around the burn pile where my son Jimmy had thrown the bones from last evening's supper. Down the hill, Old Man Gilbert was feeding the pet bull he kept on a chain. Last week the bull had broken the dog chain and pretty much ruined the old man's garden for the year, so now the bull was hooked to a log chain which snapped to a huge eyebolt anchored to the porch sill.

"He won't break that chain," Gilbert had told all the neighbors as they came one by one to mourn his ruined garden.

The pussy harness was a half-price bonus for ordering the supreme dildo. It went inside your panties and had an on/off button you kept in your pocket. It came loaded with batteries. But I didn't care nothing about the pussy harness. It was that big penis I wanted to see. Of course, except for Raymond's, and Philip's before Raymond's, and a couple of pictures one of the trashy Fleming girls had one day in high school, I had never seen very many cocks.

Jimmy Jr. proudly held up his paper.

"Look, Grandma. I'm a writing machine!"

"A what?" I answered and looked at the lines of scribbling.

"A writing machine. Mommy says one of the professors at the college says people won't need to write anything in the future, just turn on a writing machine and it will do all the writing for you."

I picked up the package and unwrapped it. I wondered if that really was Mary Alice's daughter on the late-night TV channel. What a job that would be to talk about around the Thanksgiving table. Yep, I'm selling dildos and pussy harnesses on the TV.

I dropped the package back on the table. What if Brenda, that was Mary Alice's daughter's name, what if she helped with the mailing, too, and saw my address up the holler? Oh my. I sat down with the kids and felt that fluttering in my chest again that the doctor had said was nothing to worry about. What if I had a heart attack right here and now with this package on the table? Everyone would stand around shaking their heads and muttering about how they really didn't know much about this old widow woman. How I lead this secret life. I jumped up and ran to the bathroom then tore the wrapping off the box and spilled the contents onto the floor.

It was the biggest penis imaginable. I pulled my hose and panties down and sat on the toilet. While I tinkled I licked the end of it. I tried to put my fingers around it and they wouldn't even go halfway. I propped my butt up on the seat and pushed the head of that big dick against me then laid it back in the box and pulled out the pussy harness. I pushed the button and it looked like a Cottonmouth tongue flicking out almost faster than I could see it. I had just started reading the directions when Janie May let out the awfulest scream and I dropped it on the floor, pulled up my drawers, and ran into the other room. Jimmy Jr. had her on the floor, lying on top of her, thrashing up and down.

I slapped him hard and then he was bawling along with her. I set about calming both of them down. Then here came the littlest one carrying that big dick. I snatched it away from him, went back into the bathroom where I shoved everything back in the box, and carried it into the kitchen where I opened the cupboard doors under the sink and reached into the way back. I didn't even know what was back there anymore.

As soon as I put it there I started worrying. What if I was to drop dead right now and that package was hidden there under my sink? Who would find it? Maybe the preacher's wife when she was helping to ret the house up after the funeral. Maybe Susie, looking for more scrubby pads? I imagined them staring at the massive cock and trying to figure out what the heck it was doing there and the look on their faces as they got it. Dead or not, I could not abide with either result. They would think of me for all time as a crazy, horny old woman who hid her big penis and pussy harness under the kitchen sink. Never mind that I had never used either one.

Oh, curse that cable TV.

The kids were squalling and hungry so I set about fixing sandwiches and heating up Campbell's Tomato Soup. The ham bone for our supper was done. I turned the burner off, set the bone aside, and poured the hot broth through the strainer while the soup warmed.

That evening, after our supper of ham and beans, the grandkids were playing down by the garden. Jimmy had said he would light the brush and debris from spring cleanup. He would use a tire to get it going. Susie was at the sink getting the dishes started. She could watch the kids out the window while we talked. I was just coming out of the bathroom where I had sat down and hooked up the pussy harness–I wasn't going to use it, but inside my pants seemed to be the best place I could think of to hide it–when I heard Susie shriek, the kind of blood curdling noise that mothers make when their children are in danger. I ran on out the back door to where I knew the children were. There came Gilbert's bull across the field dragging the old man's front porch. That bull had pulled the porch–sill, boards, roof and all–right off the front of the house.

Out of the corner of my eye, I saw Gilbert limping out of his yard in pursuit. That bull ran twenty more yards or so and snagged the roof on a stump. He strained and popped off most of the roof boards. Then he spied Ruthie's red t-shirt again and set off toward her. I ran as fast as I could down toward the kids. My heart was going a million miles an hour and I thought that I surely would die of a heart attack right there in the yard wearing that pussy harness.

But I couldn't stop. Those were my grandkids and I would go naked and wear that pussy harness in the Halloween Parade if it meant I could save just one of them. I could hear Susie shrieking behind me now and I heard Jimmy yell. The bull ran right through the burn pile and the framework of the porch scattered limbs and debris all over the yard. The pile slowed him down some but I saw that the bull would still get to the little ones before any of us could get there. I started bawling. The bull was thirty yards away when I heard the shot. He slowed and then there was another shot. After the third explosion that bull fell dead right in front of the kids. Gilbert had taken to never leaving the house without his Model 94 Winchester ever since that rabid skunk had attacked him several years ago. It saved the day.

We all gathered around hugging the kids. Gilbert got there, levered another round into the chamber, and shot the bull again.

"I almost killed the dumb sumbitch this morning. I wish now I had," Gilbert said.

That harness thing had activated itself while I was running and I couldn't get the button to make it turn off. It was tickling me and I kind of slapped myself in the lower tummy real quick but that pushed it a whole bunch closer to where it was supposed to be.

About that time the dog came out of the burn pile with a stick and ran over to Old Man Gilbert, who always played fetch-it with him. He threw the stick and the dog took off after it. Jimmy was gutting the bull where it lay and blood was running all over the place. Gilbert took the stick from the panting dog and reared back to throw it, but stopped and examined it.

"Well, I'll be damned," he said. "Lookee here."

"What is it?" Jimmy said.

Now I saw what had happened. The ham bone bag had broken open when the bull dragged the porch through the burn pile, and there was that dildo that I had put in with the bone.

Gilbert glanced around sheepishly and leaned close to Jimmy.

"It's a dick."

Jimmy wiped his bloody hands on the grass.

"A dick? A real one?"

"No ... an artificial one."

He held it out and Jimmy grabbed it. Then Jimmy was laughing hard.

"An artificial dick," he shouted and threw the thing for the dog to chase again.

I wanted out of there. That thing was working away in my pants, the kids were fussing at the sight of all the blood, and Susie was frowning. In the house a couple of minutes later, little Jimmy hollered out of the blue, "An artificial dick!"

I swatted his butt for him.

"Don't say that word," I said.

The grandkids started crying and I wanted everybody to go away. The next best thing was for me to hide. I went into the bedroom, shut the door, and lay down on the bed. That pussy harness was still at it, and I pushed it over a little and lay back and closed my eyes.

Johnny

After that first day of helping Kay on the door line, Johnny met her at the gate every morning and walked her to her job. His only purpose was to help a poor girl who needed him, and the only way she could get to her job without harassment from the morons in the plant was for him to walk her there. But many in the plant thought that he had other motives.

Johnny had been taught at an early age that the way to succeed was to never give up. It was that simple, his mother Tillie had taught him and his seven siblings. If you never give up, you cannot be defeated. Keep putting one foot in front of the other and you will be successful. She also taught him that the sure way to fail was through selfish motives, that goals must include goodness for others–family, friends, race, humanity–and he had become a man of compassion and humility.

During basic training, Johnny was hounded by several white recruits in his unit. He took their taunts and harassment day after day, putting one foot in front of the other, until even his drill instructor was heckling him to be a man. One hot afternoon, just after a 7-mile run, one of his tormentors tripped him from behind, kicking his leg sideways and out from under him. He thought he was injured, and lay still in the red dust. Just as the drill instructor came back the line and saw him on the ground, Johnny sprang to his feet and hit his nearest foe 5 times before the man dropped to his knees. Then he turned on the second tormentor, who was backpedaling. Left jab, right cross, left hook, left jab and the second man was down. He turned to find the rest and they were hiding behind the DI. Johnny turned from them and helped the injured Marines to their feet.

The many hundreds of hours boxing against his uncle's open palms in the cluttered living room on Friday nights or the front stoop on Sunday afternoons with all the family gathered around had given him the boxing skills he had just displayed. It was a game between Johnny and his uncle, the onetime contender passing on simple skills to a beloved nephew. And after displaying those skills that day in the red dust, Johnny was plucked out of the unit to become a Marine boxer.

One foot in front of the other. That is what had made Johnny the first black die maker in this huge stamping plant. First he was hired for production. He used to stop by the plant personnel office every Monday, Wednesday, and Friday during his lunch break from the mall down the street where he worked in janitorial. He was told hundreds of times that they weren't hiring, never told specifically they weren't hiring blacks, that they never hired blacks. But he knew that and kept coming and kept coming. Finally one day the personnel man was in a bind and would be in trouble shortly if he didn't have a "body" by the time the afternoon shift began. Johnny was ushered down to the plant hospital and given his physical, and by 3:00 pm, he was an autoworker.

Johnny had started out that first day in the same door-stacking job that Kay was assigned to now, and he knew what she was up against. After he had been stacking doors for a week, he asked a couple of men who sat all day in between the lines and occasionally got up and hit some part of a die with a hammer, or just opened a gate and brushed some scrap away from the scrap chute, what their jobs were. "Die makers," they told him. Johnny said he guessed that he would become a die maker, too.

He went to the library and studied up on die making and apprentice tests. He had always been good at math and brushed up on his skills in that area. He found sample tests and study guides for tools, shapes, and forms and spent evenings sharpening the skills he would use on the apprentice test given every spring.

When the day of the test arrived, the white shirt at the door told him he must be in the wrong place. Johnny showed him his written notice and the man was too surprised to impede him further. The guys taking the test snickered when they saw him. Black guys couldn't pass the test. Let the dumb SOB take it. Who cared?

The results were mailed out. The people who had done the grading had not known that a black man had even taken the test, and therefore did not notice that Johnny had scored high enough to become a die maker. When he showed up for apprentice orientation, he got more dirty looks than he ever remembered getting.

Management tried to prevent him from entering the room that day, but Johnny– put one foot in front of the other and seated himself. What the hell, they said, he won't make it. But

Johnny kept putting one foot in front of the other, nodding and smiling and saying "How y'all today?" to the hatred and racial slurs as he pushed his tool box down the aisle to the tool room for his first day of work. They gave him the worst jobs, put him with mean, leering, drunken leftovers of journeymen, and Johnny never let on that it was bad. As long as he could put one foot in front of the other as his mother had taught him, good things would happen. And when the die makers saw that twice a year Johnny's wife would make huge platters of barbecued chicken wings for them, that sealed the deal.

On the Monday of Kay's second week, Johnny was late in meeting her at the door. She clocked in at the time clocks along the dim hallway and looked around for Johnny. Then she heard the taunt, "Hey, nigger lover."

She had heard the words several times in the last couple of days, but never could see who was uttering them. As she glanced around seeking the source of the slur, she was pushed into a dark hallway that fed to a utility room. Two men were pressing up against her. One of them knelt beside her and tried to jerk her pants down. Kay tried to scream but could manage only a little whistle of air through her throat.

She heard a thud, like the sound of a beef roast hitting the counter in the kitchen, and one man went reeling into an air duct. The other attacker spun around and took a shot to the head and dropped. Then she saw Johnny. "Y'all shouldn't have done that," he said, and helped Kay to her feet, turning her away from the two.

A couple of minutes later, when she had straightened her clothing and was calm enough to continue on, the two of them entered the bright hallway. "Hey, nigger lover," they both heard.

Johnny knew that he had to quit walking her to her job, and when they reached the first break area, he sat her down and told her that. She looked at his kind face and nodded, trying to squeeze off the tears as they formed.

"This is an ugly, stupid place," he said.

She nodded through her tears.

"There is no sense to any of it here," he continued. "Do you have your apron?"

She plopped the folded oil cloth apron he had made onto the table. "Thank you."

"Do you have your safety glasses?" he asked and stood up. "One foot in front of the other, okay?" And then he was gone.

When Kay got to the door line that morning, she was met by the foreman, who told her she was being transferred to the quarter panel line. She was upset at first—her job stacking doors might have been hell, but it was her hell and she had survived it. She wasn't sure what other horrors this place might hold. But she did as she was told and when she turned to leave, the man in the white shirt said, "Good luck."

She turned back to him. Good luck? This person who had seemed like her personal tormenter wished her well?

"It was nothing personal," he said. "This place …" and he shrugged his shoulders and shouted at the new girl taking her place on the door line.

This place, Kay said to herself as she turned away. She took one last look and pitied the young black lady, a new hire, taking her place. But the feeling was momentary–it was either her, or the new hire, at the end of that line from hell. She turned and marched along the front of the press lines, the booming of the draw dies drowning out the catcalls of the men in the plant.

A Bad Thing

The angry roar and hiss of the factory fill the air. A cherry bomb goes off behind Bobby Finnegan. He flinches at the explosion, five feet from him, and he lets loose of his share of the roof panel and watches it settle onto the trim die, then steps back as Eddie cycles the press with the lone pair of palm buttons. There is a tremendous crunch as the press bottoms out and the scrap pieces clatter down the scrap chutes or onto the floor, to be kicked or shoved down the chutes later when there is a lull in the action. And then, whoosh, he can feel the air as a rolled up pair of cotton gloves whizzes past his face. Down the line a plastic sandwich bag filled with water hits the press face and splatters over the guys manning that press.

Bobby hurries back to the draw press, which has just boomed and exploded another huge piece of sheet metal into the form of a car roof. Then he and his partner, Eddie Smoad, reach into the die, well, not really into it, since putting any part of your body in a pinch point is grounds for firing, and drag the heavy panel out and tip it up so that they can get both hands on it, one hand clamped tightly to keep the panel from slipping and slicing to the bone through the thin, cotton gloves. Bobby and Eddie are in a rhythm, running at times back and forth between their press and the big, lead toggle press, which is capable of cycling every eight seconds.

They load another huge panel and the men step back, two more of them on the other side of the press waiting to take the trimmed roof panel on to the next press. Like a huge game of leap frog, there are four men between presses, two cycling the press and two going back upstream to get the roof panel out of the prior die, alternating job positions.

Bobby and Eddie grab another panel out of the greasy draw die, and a shower of cotton glove balls rains down on them. One of them hits Bobby in the side of the face, knocking his safety glasses part way off. It won't be long until he can return fire; he knows who threw that one and now he owes him. Bobby and Eddie load the panel, step back, and the monstrous trim die crunches another one. Then Bobby sees his chance; there are a half dozen glove balls on the die shoe, and he grabs two of them and wheels around, preparing to fire as his torso rotates, when he slips in the oil that has dripped from the roof panels and the press all morning.

Bobby can hear the press movement and wonders at that. That is what he always would remember, the press cycling when it wasn't supposed to. Bobby stops himself from falling into the scrap chute, with his back against the lower die shoe and his left arm on the die adaptor, and can feel the rough cast iron sliding, as if in slow motion, down the back of his head, remembers it touching his shoulder, and hears the ka-lump as the die bottoms without metal in it, and the huge die pad settles itself.

Dazed, Bobby stands leaning against the press bed and die shoe, thankful that he had not fallen down the scrap chute or into the die. Then Eddie is screaming, and something doesn't feel right to Bobby, and it is then he notices the big red splotch in the roof die, and sees the bone fragments hanging along the trim edge of the die adaptor, looking like the metal slivers that sometimes build up when the trim steels are getting dull. Bobby releases the glove balls onto the floor and watches as one of them bounces down the scrap chute. Then the pain comes like a deep, evil fog, and Bobby sees that his left arm is gone from his biceps on down.

Cranston Journal editor Tom Finnegan was alone in the newsroom as he imagined the day of his brother Bobby's accident yet another time. This was the way Tom always pieced it together. There was the oil on the floor that Bobby had explained made him fall. Usually there was a guy assigned to mop up the oil and panel lube every hour, but Bobby's area was shorthanded that day and went without. Then there was the horseplay –the firecrackers, glove balls, water bags, fire extinguisher fights – it was just the way the place was, a way to break the monotony and stupidity of the simple yet brutal atmosphere in the plant. But more importantly and strangely was the press cycling when it did, the feared "random cycle" that can happen anytime on a press and which is something most people can spend a lifetime in a pressroom and never witness.

In the hospital, Bobby kept high spirits. His wife and babies were there every day to see him, and they, after all, were what his life was about. What more could a good Catholic boy from a large Catholic family need but family?

And taking care of your family was everything–putting the food on the table and the dresses on his two pretty, red-headed daughters and a smile on wife Katie's face. When she had gotten pregnant in the spring of their senior year, Bobby didn't hesitate–they got married with a gay, spring church wedding full of pretty little nieces and serious little nephews carrying flowers and rings and more. The baby was just a little bit early was all anyone needed to know, and that was good enough.

Tom Finnegan gazed out his office door at the rows of typewriters and composing tables in the newsroom. When it was quiet here it was such an unnatural state for the place, usually filled with the clack-clacking of the typewriters and the bustle of young folks hustling copy here and there to the editors or layout or composing. He wondered if it had gotten quiet at the factory the day Bobby lost his arm. He thought not, that the monster of a plant, always working people seven days a week, holidays, holy days, everyday, would surely not take notice of the blood and bone of a young man who was still a little boy to Tom Finnegan, the oldest of the Finnegan clan of nine children. No, the plant did not pause for Bobby Finnegan.

He was writing an editorial for the Sunday paper about the General Motors stamping plant. The day before, for the Thanksgiving Day edition, he had written the headline for the wildcat strike of Wednesday: "Once Again: Violence Strikes." Tom Finnegan found it amusing, if sardonically so, to listen to the other community leaders speak of the money spigot that the GM plant was to them. No one could deny the benefit of the multimillion-dollar payroll the plant provided or the tax that payroll generated for the school system. If General Motors had required the annual sacrifice of a virgin, it is likely that the Chamber of Commerce would have okayed it, with the stipulation, as with all things requiring sacrifice, that the virgin come from the other side of the tracks, or even better, be imported.

At the Chamber or Kiwanis or country club, he heard over and over what ingrates the uneducated masses working at the plant were. A wildcat strike was illegal. Call in the National Guard. Show them who is boss. Tom used to try to present an opposing view, the actual reality of the plant, the working conditions of the job, and the disregard for human rights by GM, but they always laughed him off as a raving Irishman who needed to be getting on with his life, that it was his granddaddy who had fled the potato famine and, "Pinch yourself, Tom, you are the editor of a very large American newspaper." But they didn't know his little brother, or, if they had, could not remember him. They could not comprehend that Bobby had taken a forty cent an hour cut in pay from his job bagging groceries at Big Bear to go to GM, and that the only reason the men made good wages was because of the overtime. Bobby didn't work it all, and he still averaged seventy hours a week.

Only one person from the plant had at first been involved when Bobby lost his arm, a young fellow named Milt Jeffers, Bobby's union representative. "We're just getting the paperwork right," he told Bobby's wife, and Tom Finnegan, who happened to be in the hospital room that evening. "I expect the first check will be cut in a few days and we'll get started on rehab." They all thanked Milt, and he went on his way.

Fuck, there was nothing the young Milt Jeffers could do. Deals were always being made, but he wasn't yet the dealmaker. First the company said Bobby violated shop rule #3 about putting any body part in a die pinch point. Then they said it was horseplay, a violation of shop rule #27. But the strangest thing was the random press cycle. For sure, Eddie had not cycled the press; there were enough eyes in the area to know that for sure. A General Motors press just cycles and takes off a man's arm.

The day the registered letter came from GM, Bobby was in good spirits. Just he and Katie and the girls were in the room, and Bobby was getting ready to go home the next day. He tore open the envelope and scanned its contents. The color was gone from his face when he tucked it away and turned back to Katie and their plans. Later when Katie had gone for the day, he took the envelope out and read the letter again. He was fired! GM had fired him for horseplay, which caused his accident!

Tom had helped Bobby in dealing with the company, most of it through Milt Jeffers. He was dumbfounded at the outcome. Bobby was permanently disabled and unable to work, and GM had fired him? The personnel director refused to see him. The shop chairman at the time, along with Milt Jeffers in a meeting, said the matter was in step two, and explained the lengthy grievance procedure. Ultimately, it did not matter about the steps. A month later, Katie found Bobby in the basement. He had set a folding chair near the floor drain, removed the drain cover, and tilted his head back before shooting himself through the mouth.

Goosy Gus and the Cash Mob

Gus had acquired the name "Goosy" because of his battle fatigue from WWII and now he was no longer allowed in his daughter-in-law's donut shop in downtown Cranston even though eating donuts was his favorite way to start the day.

When he was cornered or confronted with loud noises, he struck or grabbed the people or things in proximity to himself. All who knew him tried not to surprise him, though the guys at the steel mill used to enjoy getting him going. One day the new mill manager was touring the plant and introducing himself to the employees and when he came to Gus, one of the other millwrights slammed a board down on the floor behind Gus. The result was that Gus grabbed the plant manager by the throat and squeezed. He almost got fired over that one, until the security department and plant hospital confirmed Gus's disability to Human Resources.

The reason he was barred from the donut shop was because of the "Buy Local" campaign, a last ditch save-our-jobs-and-city effort spearheaded by the local corporate newspaper. The same paper that had scoffed at Gus's Buy American letters to the editor twenty years earlier when American workers like him were pleading with the American people to consider buying union products made here in the USA.

Goosy Gus had been there eating a maple-frosted cake donut one morning when two carloads of folks–the newspaper editor included–piled out of a couple of Toyota vans and came into the shop, babbling about the big comeback the downtown area was experiencing.

As they all ordered bags of donuts the daughter-in-law realized she was the benefactor of this week's Cash Mob, a group of do-gooders who bought shit from a targeted merchant on a certain day.

Gus sat in the corner sizing them up.

There was the editor, whom Gus referred to as a con artist and fraud and said that if journalism was a spitball it wouldn't stick to his slippery ass. The head of the Chamber of Commerce was there too, a country clubber of the highest order who had sided with the national Chamber and Karl Rove in spending $40 million to try and beat Ohio Senator Sherrod Brown.

Along with those two was a gaggle of hangers-on, the sort that Gus knew from looking had never worked a day in their lives. These folks were all here to shower some welfare on his daughter-in-law's store.

Gus sank low in his chair at the back table, hoping this too happy group would buy their donuts and get out. He had just received notice that his health insurance, part of his steel mill retirement from a decade earlier, was being terminated and he was in no mood to hear about the happy horseshit these folks were shoveling.

With no warning the company had dropped his insurance. There was a meeting scheduled for that afternoon at the union hall, but Gus knew there was nothing anyone could do about it. The company always won. They would fake bankruptcy, lie, cheat, steal, buy politicians and newspaper editors, whatever it took. Goosy Gus had only wanted to consume a maple donut in silence–two this morning instead of his usual one–to soothe some of the pain he was feeling. He knew that with his wife's medical bills his savings would be gone in another four months, and he, along with a bunch of the other retirees would be headed on a shit-greased slippery slope to bankruptcy.

Facing bankruptcy, and this chicken-shit corporate newspaper editor and his thieving business leader buddy were all gallivanting around the decayed remnants of the downtown with a bunch of old women who had never hit a lick in their lives, babbling about how great it all was that donut and basket shops were springing up in the ruins.

One of these women got Gus banned from the donut shop. She had gulped two Percocets from her new prescription that morning and was cackling like a rooster pheasant on opening day.

Gus had heard her jabbering from curbside when the do-gooders first got there. Then when they entered the store she gushed and eyed the pastries, pointing out the various kinds and describing them in detail, dashing around in front of the other Cash Mob People.

Now she was in front of Gus's table–the lone occupied table in the place–gesturing at the donuts in the glass case and on the shelves behind his daughter-in-law, pointing at him, then to the donuts and people nearby. He heard the words "Buy Local" and "Cash Mob" several times. He watched the cackling woman, her husband was a bank vice president and they went to his church–Gus's church not their church–as they were fresh in from the out-of-town corporate merry-go-round like all the people who now owned everything in his town, folks he called Transients. As her face grew red and heated through her speed-freak dance before his table, he stood up and tried to slide along the wall toward the exit but she followed right along with him. He couldn't help noticing her nipples pressed hard against the front of her rust-colored silk blouse, growing in unison with her dance. He fixated on them as they grew longer and sharper and pointed as if accusing him of some undefined crime.

Gus thought about the expensive silk blouse she was wearing. Sexually abused little girls in South America probably made it. The union had always made sure its members were educated on the issue of global labor, and Gus knew about maquiladoras.

Gus heard the words "Cash Mob" and "Buy Local" one more time. His right hand shot out in a blur of motion. His calloused and swollen arthritic fingers latched on to her left elongated nipple. He twisted it to the right. She screamed. She screamed several times. The Buy

Local mob members turned toward Gus as the lady backed away, pointing at Goosy Gus.

Gus's daughter-in –law had been the only person to see what had happened, and as she realized that none of the others had seen it, that they were all intent on her delicious donuts, she did not rat out her husband's father, despicable throwback that he was.

The woman calmed down, but kept Gus in her view. She rejoined the group, and in a couple more minutes the Cash Mob was gone. Gus's daughter-in-law stood over him at the table. She shook her head in silence as he finished his coffee.

"Fucking Toyota drivers," Goosy Gus said.

Now every morning Goosy Gus sat at the Dunkin' Donuts out by the freeway. For a while he said, "I like Dunkin' Donuts better anyways" until his son told him to shut the fuck up.

The Last Easter Egg Hunt
November, 2008

The dozen GM Cranston retirees sit four to a yellow vinyl booth, like passengers on a train, craning their necks to join in the conversation from the other booths. The row of tables next to the booths fills with the other dozen old men who are joining them. They are survivors, appreciative of the resilience of the human liver, or cognizant by now of the importance of good genes. They have made it through the gauntlet of workplace injuries and diseases, boredom, mental and physical fatigue, and emerged in retirement.

As a group, their aura is gray, born of their thirty, forty, fifty years of oil mist, grinding dust, and welder smoke. The heat treat man has a red leathery face from his decades of leaning over two-thousand-degree oven pits. The press operators sit calmly like well-trained dogs, as if the bondage to the press lines still exists, and they are awaiting orders from either the boss or the movement of parts toward them. The die makers wear porous faces turned pallid from the daily barrage of abrasive materials.

The talk is of the upcoming interview with Rick Wagoner, CEO of General Motors, and Ron Gettelfinger, the United Auto Workers International President. The retirees glance at the television hung on the lime green wall at the end of the seating area, as if their future hangs with it. They are watching the financial channel, CNBC. The ticker line displays the current value of GM stock, at its lowest valuation in fifty years. Toyota could write a check for $2.5 billion and own the whole mess – all the hundreds of factories around the world, along with the name brands of Chevrolet, GMC, Pontiac, Buick, Cadillac, and Saturn. Later in the day will be the Easter Egg Hunt on the front lawn of the plant, the last scheduled joint activity to be hosted by the local entities of General Motors and the United Auto Workers. No matter that it is November –hundreds of children will dash across the front lawn one last time, scooping up plastic eggs filled with prize certificates from local merchants who, one more time, had coughed up tens of thousands of dollars for the annual Easter Egg Hunt.

The men had stood on picket lines

together, carried their wounded and dead out of the jumble of press lines on stretchers, and worked uncountable hours of overtime to get through model changeover in the heyday of GM. These old men would go out to the plant and watch the grandchildren that were their legacies, the flesh and blood that had commanded their bondage to rows of machinery most of their adult lives, scurry after plastic Easter egg prizes.

The ticker crawls across the bottom of the screen as CNBC's announcer, somber yet cheerfull recounts the demise of the American auto giant. The men watch the symbols of stocks they once owned or now own through their retirement accounts–all, it seems, worth a small fraction of what they paid for them. The stock market did not treat any of them well, though it is something they do not talk about. None of them would admit that they had been hoodwinked by a government and economic elite that had convinced all of America to put its money in the stock market to be harvested as fast as human gullibility would allow by the day-trading experts on Wall Street. None of them would admit to faring any worse than "breaking even" in the stock market, though most of them had lost ninety per cent of their retirement savings.

Bob Elliot enters the diner, and the men at the tables begin shuffling their chairs to make room for the man. Bob was the manager of the Cranston plant for twenty years after John Dunham was promoted in the late seventies. He guided the plant through the tumult of the eighties and was considered the reason for the plant's longstanding success. Elliot had planned to stay in Cranston only a couple of years before being promoted to GM vice-president, but some things happened which pitted him against the top brass–mainly, after the two years in Cranston, he was told that his ticket to Detroit would be shutting down the plant. He told them to go to hell, and dug in and fortified the Cranston plant, pulling in all his favors from around the country to increase the workload and job security at his plant. In short, he declared war against the GM system. And it had worked until his retirement ten years ago. Only now, thirty years after it first tried, was GM successful in shutting down his beloved plant.

"Hey, Bob," calls one retiree, and the others give their greetings or nod to this man they all respect. There had not been a constant union/management problem during the years that

Bob ran the plant. He made it clear through his actions that he was one of them–if they failed, they would all fail together, all go down together. When all was said and done, Bob was a working man like they were.

Then Wagoner and Gettelfinger are on the TV. "We are on the verge of bankruptcy," Wagoner begins. "The next one hundred days will determine if we survive. Sales are down fifty per cent since gas prices doubled and the Wall Street bailout began. We need a short term loan ... if we can pledge a trillion dollars to the banking industry, we think it is fair that we are loaned this money ...."

The CNBC announcer interrupts, "Why should we give you any money? Foreign car makers are doing okay in the south."

"They were subsidized by the states," Gettelfinger says.

"Isn't that how it works?"

"When tax abatements first started in the 70's, the UAW warned of their consequences," the union president continues.

"Isn't the truth of the matter that GM has been mismanaged?"

"You know better than that," Wagoner says. The jaw muscles tighten in his face. Just once he would like to tell these people what was what. Sure, mistakes had been made ....

"Aren't your labor agreements the problem?" the announcer asks.

"No, no, no," Gettelfinger answers. "Labor amounts to ten per cent of the vehicle cost. Our government looked the other way when foreign governments manipulated their currencies to gain market share in America. It was our own government that sold GM out with NAFTA ...."

"Sorry, we're out of time," the guy on CNBC bellows. "Ladies and gentlemen, Rick Wagoner from GM and Ron Gettelfinger from the UAW. Thanks for being here."

"Turn that shit off," one of the guys hollers. Then the waitress is bringing their eggs and bacon and fried potatoes. They eat in silence, the impending bankruptcy of their company and the end of their retirement pay and benefits looming. There are a few attempts at humor or reviving a story or two from the old days, but nothing takes hold.

When the waitress brings the checks, the heat treat man grabs the plant manager's. "Your money's no good here today, Bob." In a few minutes they have paid their bills and filed out of the restaurant, where a few of them linger talking in the parking lot.

A convoy of lowboy flatbeds snakes around the plant. Every couple of hours, a loaded truck groans away from the shipping docks and onto Route 30 with press beds and motors, lathes and mills, and fork lifts and tow motors, all on their way to new owners who bought them at auction several months ago. There is no way to stop the procession of movers, men making a living dragging away the remnants of other men's lives.

A thousand people pack the front lawn of the stamping plant. There are the children, making their way to the starting line, the parents and grandparents, and the plant management along with the union officers, all together this one last time.

Then a whistle signals the beginning, and the children dash onto the prize-covered field. The boys and girls fill their donated, plastic Walmart bags with the prizes, all of them finding success as there are thousands of eggs scattered on the lawn. On the far side, a couple of children race along, scooping the eggs into their bags.

When the smaller of the two reaches for a large egg, he is sent reeling across the lawn by the other boy. The boy sits up, his prizes scattered before him. He looks around to get his bearings, and sees his transgressor picking up the eggs that spilled out of his bag. He rushes over and confronts him.

"Those are my eggs."

"You dropped them. They're mine now."

The cheers from the parents and grandparents drift across to the two. The younger boy looks around and then back to the boy. "There's eggs everywhere. Just go on and leave mine alone."

The bigger boy steps forward and shoves him. "You don't get it, do you? My dad's management. He owns this plant. He'll always be in charge. And so will I someday."

The younger boy doesn't understand what the other is saying. He glances across the field to where his dad and grandpa are standing. They both worked here. Didn't they maybe own some of the place, too?

The boy starts scooping up the rest of the spilled eggs. "Go on now. Or I'll push you down again."

The boy hits the other as he has been

taught–with his fist, on the eye, and as hard as he can.

The older boy sinks to his knees, sobbing now as he fingers his already swelling eye. "You hurt me …."

The smaller boy takes both egg-filled bags and backs away. "Fuck you," he says. "I've got all the eggs now."

Time

I saw a man yesterday standing on the freshly constructed wheelchair walkway of a little square house. The walkway was made of treated lumber and went two zigs and one zag until it reached the front door.

He stood in the middle of it all, a man of about seventy, gazing calmly at the cars that passed by, one about every thirty seconds. He watched each car, with neither malice or even curiosity, as if he were looking for the sake of the observation, seeing who might be traveling by the little house on this sunny, but cold and windy day in April.

If I were to write his story, I would say that he labored mightily, with the help of his sons and grandsons, to build this ramp for his father, who was ninety something and died a day after its completion. I would write that I have seen his expression before, that blankness that is beyond the crying, that look of calmness of surrender that humans wear after a death sinks in. I would write that he will proceed bravely into his last decade or two, because he has children and grandchildren and there are many things he can help them with, too, before he needs some help of his own.

William Trent Pancoast

1949—

"Blue collar writer" is how the *Wall Street Journal* referred to William Trent Pancoast in a 1986 front page article. By that time, his working-class-flavored short stories and essays had appeared in many midwestern and international magazines and newspapers. Pancoast's novel *Crashing* had been published in 1983. In 1986, his United Auto Workers union history was published. Pancoast spent the next twenty years as the editor of a monthly union newspaper—the *Union Forum*—while continuing to publish his fiction, essays, and editorials in the *Union Forum, Solidarity* magazine, *US News and World Report*, and numerous literary magazines.

After he retired in 2006, he wrote *Wildcat* and it was published in 2010. In 2016 he revised and reissued *Crashing* in paperback. In 2017 he published *The Road To Matewan*, a book he started in 1972 and was able to finally complete.

The term "blue collar writer" suits Pancoast just fine. As he said in the *WSJ* interview, "The reason I write about work is that that's just about damn near all I've ever done." In addition to his jobs of die maker, machinist, railroad section hand and brakeman, and construction laborer, Pancoast has been a high school English teacher and adjunct professor of English. The author supplements his blue collar writing credentials with a B.A. in English from the Ohio State University.

Pancoast is retired from the auto industry after thirty years as a die maker and union newspaper editor and lives in Ontario, Ohio.